SQUEEZE PLAY

Frank wandered over to take a closer look at the doorway of the gallery. On either side, steel panels were set into the walls so skillfully that he would not have noticed them if his father hadn't pointed them out. He reached out to feel the cool, smooth edge of one of them.

Without warning a horn blared deafeningly. From the corners of the room, floodlights blazed into life.

Frank whirled around. His father's face showed sheer disbelief. Then, as he glanced in Frank's direction, his expression changed abruptly to terror.

"Frank, the doors!" he shouted. "You'll be crushed!"

Frank looked over his shoulder as the two giant steel doors, like the jaws of some hungry beast, thundered toward him.

Books in THE HARDY BOYS CASEFILES℠ Series

Available from ARCHWAY Paperbacks

THE HARDY BOYS
CASEFILES
NO. 84

FALSE ALARM

FRANKLIN W. DIXON

AN ARCHWAY PAPERBACK
Published by POCKET BOOKS
New York   London   Toronto   Sydney   Tokyo   Singapore

AN ARCHWAY PAPERBACK *Original*

An Archway Paperback published by
POCKET BOOKS, a division of Simon & Schuster Inc.
1230 Avenue of the Americas, New York, NY 10020

Copyright © 1994 by Simon & Schuster Inc.
Produced by Mega-Books of New York, Inc.

ISBN: 0-671-79468-X

First Archway Paperback printing February 1994

10 9 8 7 6 5 4 3 2 1

THE HARDY BOYS, AN ARCHWAY PAPERBACK and colophon are registered trademarks of Simon & Schuster Inc.

THE HARDY BOYS CASEFILES is a trademark of Simon & Schuster Inc.

Cover art by Brian Kotzky

Printed in the U.S.A.

IL 6+

FALSE ALARM

Chapter

1

BILL MATTHEWS, Bayport High School's wrestling coach, gave a short blast on his whistle. "Hardy? Moreno?" he called. "You're up."

Seventeen-year-old Joe Hardy clasped his hands, stretched them over his head, then rolled his shoulders to loosen them. His wavy blond hair fell onto his forehead. Brushing it back, he stepped onto the wrestling mat, opposite Vince Moreno. A deep breath apiece, a shriek from the coach's whistle, and they were grappling.

Vince was good, but Joe knew he was better. His muscles straining, Joe pushed to the right, then pulled back to the left trying for the leverage he needed. Outside, a cold February wind

1

was blowing, but with his effort Joe felt sweat beading on his forehead.

The match wasn't the Olympics, but it mattered all the same. That day's round-robin match was the first of the wrestling practice season, and Coach Matthews was going to use the results to work out the positions on the team. Joe had been number one the year before, and he was determined to hold on to his rank.

"Unh!" Joe grunted as Vince grabbed him around the waist to pull him off balance. Joe hooked his right foot behind Vince's knee and threw his weight forward. The two wrestlers crashed to the mat. Joe twisted like a cat while falling and not giving his opponent an instant to recover, pinned him to the mat.

Coach Matthews dropped to his hands and knees next to them and started the count. "One! Two! Three!"

He slapped Joe on the shoulder. "Okay, Hardy. You got him."

Joe bounced to his feet and gave Vince a hand up. "Good round," he said as the other wrestlers applauded from the bleachers.

Vince tugged the sweat band off his long, dark hair. "Thanks, Joe. Good luck against that new guy. He's built like a tank."

Joe glanced over at the bleachers. Front and center sat his next opponent, a sophomore named Ed Mason, who was new to the team and to Bayport. Ed was short, with a stubby nose, perfectly styled brown hair, and sharply defined muscles bulging everywhere. He and his brother, Peter, had moved to Bayport from California over the Christmas holidays, so Joe hand't yet seen Ed in action. The coach had, and was already talking up his strength and solid technique.

From the sidelines, Frank Hardy called out, "Say cheese, guys." Joe turned just in time to get a strobe flash in the face.

Frank, a year older and an inch taller than Joe, slung his camera over his shoulder, then handed Joe a cup of water and a towel. "Good fall," he said to Joe as Vince strode off toward the bleachers. "If the pictures come out, maybe the yearbook will use a couple. We've got to show posterity that we did more in high school than chase crooks."

Joe wiped his face and took a sip of water. "Good idea," he said. "Right now chasing crooks seems like a breeze."

The coach blew his whistle again. "Okay, boys," he said, studying his clipboard. "Next up are Johnson and Pollack, then Hardy and Mason."

"Mason, eh?" Frank said, turning his camera on the bleachers. "You mean the kid in the body-builder shirt over there?"

Again Frank's strobe flashed, and Ed Mason

blinked owlishly at the light. Then he got to his feet and crossed the gym toward the Hardys.

"Right," Joe murmured, keeping his eye on Mason. "He may be a year younger than I am, but I have a feeling he's experienced for his age."

"Yo! I hope you'll give me a copy of that pic, Mr. Photographer." Ed Mason joined Frank and Joe as Johnson and Pollack faced off on the mat behind them.

"You bet," Frank replied cheerfully. "But you can call me Frank. And this is my kid brother, Joe Hardy—the guy you're challenging for first position." Frank shook hands with Ed, who introduced himself, adding, "You'd better watch out for Joe. He eats wrestlers for breakfast."

Ed turned to Joe as though he'd just noticed him and gave him a critical once-over. "It shows, too much red meat," he said in an arrogant tone of voice. "You know, Joe, balanced meals are really important in this sport. The right diet and a well-planned weight program are what it takes to be a champion."

Joe blinked. This guy figures he's already number one, he thought angrily. Why does he think he can give me advice? Joe forced a friendly grin to his face and said, half-joking, "Wait till you see what a few pepperoni slices from Mr. Pizza and a little nap do for me. Maybe I can offer you a mat sandwich."

Frank jumped in. "Don't mind Joe," he said to Ed. "He's just pumping himself up for his match with you."

"Hey, whatever works," Ed replied. "I know some people need that to make themselves feel big."

With that, Ed turned and sauntered off toward the weight benches across the gym. With half-closed eyes he began doing a series of curls with two dumbbells. He was impressive before he started, but after a minute his muscles really pumped up and even Joe had to admit that Ed Mason was *built*.

"This round-robin just got a lot more interesting," Joe remarked to his brother. "There's one stuck-up sophomore I can't wait to beat."

The second match was over in two falls, and then it was Joe and Ed's turn. Coach Matthews's excitement showed as the two competitors stepped onto the mat. He was obviously pleased to have another top-notch wrestler on his team, as well as curious about which of them was better.

"We've got time for only one fall, gentlemen," he said. "So make it your best."

Joe knew that this was one of the coach's favorite pressure tactics. It really tightened the screws to know that there wasn't time for a single careless move. Joe was used to it, and it didn't seem to faze Ed, either.

Joe grabbed the first hold, an arm lock that the shorter boy broke easily. Ed's muscles weren't just big, they were hard.

The fall stretched out as each in turn reached for holds that the other broke with a combination of strength, talent, and willpower. Ed wrestled with a ferocity that took Joe aback. This was a practice match, not life or death.

All at once Ed reached down, grabbed Joe's ankle, and twisted, as one powerful shoulder thunked into Joe's abdomen. Nothing apparently illegal, but the *way* his ankle twisted was something that Joe had never experienced before. The move wasn't clean wrestling.

Pain shot up Joe's leg. His breath exploded as Ed pinned him to the mat. The count was over before Joe knew what had happened.

"That's it! Mason's fall!"

The muscular newcomer got up with a self-satisfied smile on his face. Some teammates clustered around to congratulate him. Joe closed his eyes and gritted his teeth, fighting back the humiliation.

"Hey, Joe, are you okay?" Frank demanded, kneeling down next to him.

Joe tried to reply, but all that came out was a groan.

*   *   *

After practice Frank was helping Joe back to their lockers when they ran into Vanessa Bender.

"Joe, what happened?" she asked, concerned about his taped-up ankle.

"It got twisted the wrong way," Joe replied. "Coach says a few days of soaking in hot water and Epsom salts, and it'll be good as new."

"That's a relief," Vanessa said, tucking her arm into his. "I hate to think what the other guy must look like."

"He's looking pretty good," Frank said. "The fact is, he won. It's hard to believe, but there just might be someone better than Joe on the wrestling team."

"I'm telling you," Joe said through clenched teeth, "there was something fishy about that move he made. I don't think it was an accident."

"Well, the coach didn't call a foul," Frank pointed out. "I'm sorry you got beat, Joe—but you *did* get beat. Once your ankle's better, you can try to beat him again."

Vanessa wrapped a lock of her ash blond hair around a forefinger. "I don't think you're going to be in any shape for a day of hiking on Saturday," she said thoughtfully.

Joe slapped his forehead. "The Winter Charity Hike! But we're all signed up!" He was so upset that he put too much weight on his injured

7

ankle. If Frank hadn't grabbed him, he would have fallen.

"It'll be okay," Vanessa said. "That new guy, Ed Mason, was asking me this morning if I had a partner for the hike. I told him I did and promised to dig one up for him. Now it looks as though *I* need a partner, so that all works out."

"Ed Mason?" Joe felt as if he were about to fall over again.

"Right," Vanessa said. "Have you met him? He's a great guy, Joe. Lots of energy. Knows an amazing amount about diet and health. I bet he could do wonders for that ankle of yours."

"He already did," Joe said sourly. "He's the one who twisted it for me."

Vanessa stared at him. "Really? That's awful! I can't imagine that he hurt you on purpose."

Joe pressed his lips together. What could he do? If he slammed Ed, Vanessa would probably decide that he was jealous. The charity hike wasn't exactly a date, and it was for a good cause. There was no chance he was going to be able to walk six miles the day after next.

Vanessa went on tiptoes to give Joe a peck on the cheek. "I'd better run," she said. "Mom's expecting me for dinner. I hope you feel better, Joe." As she walked away, she yelled back over her shoulder, "Give me a call tonight."

As soon as she was out of earshot, Joe growled, "Ed Mason! First, he steals my place on the team and busts my ankle. Now he's trying to steal Vanessa, too!"

"You've got it backward," Frank remarked. "He asked Vanessa about the hike *before* he had his match with you. Before he'd even met you, for that matter. And he didn't steal your place on the team, he won it."

"Whose side are you on, anyway?" Joe burst out. "Mine or that phony's?"

"Come off it, Joe," Frank replied sharply. "There's nothing phony about those muscles of his. You should know that better than anyone."

"Yeah, he has great muscles, but I'll handle him next time," Joe retorted. "Better than you'll be able to handle competition from *Peter* Mason."

Joe knew this was a cheap shot, but it hit home. Peter, Ed's older brother, was said to have a huge IQ. People around school were already talking about the new high school senior's project for the spring science fair. Nobody knew exactly what it was, but it had something to do with robotics, something that would make Frank's miniaturized forensics lab look like a kindergarten project.

"Cybernetics and robotics go over big with judges, it's true," Frank said ruefully. "But I'm not doing my project to win a prize, you know. It's something we'll be able to use all the time."

"Maybe so, but I've got a feeling this is going

to be a rough semester,'' Joe said as he limped down the hall.

Back home Frank and Joe headed for the kitchen to get a snack.

Their father, the internationally known private detective Fenton Hardy, lay slumped over the kitchen table.

"Dad!" Joe exclaimed, trying to rush forward.

Frank grabbed his shoulder. "Hold it, Joe," he whispered. "Dad's okay. Check out his breathing. He's just catching a nap. He's been having a pretty rough week, you know."

Joe paused. "Oh—right," he said in a low voice. "The Bayport Museum job."

Frank nodded. "It's not easy being in charge of the security setup for fifty million dollars' worth of jewels. From what Dad's said, there are a bunch of problems he wasn't expecting."

"The crown jewels of Botrovia. Sounds like something out of an old detective thriller," said Joe. He took the milk carton from the refrigerator, then peered inside, to see if any of their aunt Gertrude's chocolate cream pie was left over.

"It is pretty thrilling," Frank said. "You know, until recently Botrovia was a part of the Soviet Union, and the jewels haven't been out of the country for years. I'm really looking forward to seeing them."

The door behind them swung open. They

whirled around to see their aunt Gertrude pointing an accusing finger at Joe. "Get your nose out of that refrigerator, young man," she ordered. "I've got a nice pot roast in the oven, and I won't have you ruining your supper!"

"Shhh!" Joe said. "Dad's asleep." He glanced over, but his father hadn't stirred.

"Oh, for heaven's sake," Gertrude Hardy said. "You'd think a grown man would have enough sense to lie down when he needs a nap."

"He's been working pretty much around the clock," Frank explained. "Maybe we'd better—"

Without warning an electronic shriek went off. Fenton Hardy sprang to his feet, his chair crashing to the floor behind him.

"The jewels!" he shouted wildly. "Somebody's trying to steal the jewels!"

Chapter

2

FENTON RUSHED to the wall phone and tapped out a number. After a short exchange, he hung up and turned to face the others in the kitchen.

"I can't believe it," he said, shaking his head. "Another false alarm."

"What's going on, Dad?"

Fenton pressed his fingertips to his eyes and rubbed for a moment. "It's that new security system we've installed at the museum. It's a custom version of the Hawk 9–2000 Mega System."

"That's about the most sensitive system around, isn't it," Frank remarked.

"Maybe a little *too* sensitive," his father replied. "Ever since we installed it, it's been going off several times a day, for no reason at all."

"You need a nice cup of warm milk," Aunt Gertrude said, moving to the microwave with a mug of cold milk.

"A problem with the hardware, Dad?" Frank suggested. "Or maybe a bug in the programming?"

Fenton tightened his lips in a straight line, then said, "You'd think so, wouldn't you? But I've had a team of analysts running diagnostics until they're blue in the face. They say everything in the system is working the way it's supposed to."

He returned to his chair and slumped down as Gertrude Hardy put a steaming mug of hot milk in front of him. "The guards are worn out," he continued. "And as for the Bayport police, we've hollered wolf so many times, I don't think they'd respond if a pack of wolves surrounded the museum and started baying at the moon in four-part harmony!"

"Can't you just install a different system?" asked Joe.

"A system as good as we need? In a matter of days? Impossible." He drained the mug and stood up again. "I'm going to hit the hay," he announced. "Maybe things will look more cheerful in the morning."

"What about dinner?" Aunt Gertrude asked.

"Just put it in the fridge for me," he replied. "I'll have it for breakfast."

Moments later they heard his footsteps on the stairs.

"Pot roast for breakfast. Sounds radical," Joe remarked.

"How can you make jokes when your father is clearly at his wit's end?" Aunt Gertrude demanded.

Frank shrugged. "I wouldn't worry. Dad's pretty resourceful. And besides, he's probably right. Things will seem better in the morning."

Frank was very aware of the clatter of trays and silverware and the loud hum of conversation in the cafeteria as he peered around.

"There's Vanessa now," Frank said.

Joe raised his head eagerly. "Where?"

"In the lunch line," Frank replied, grinning. "You didn't sprain your neck, too, did you?"

Callie Shaw put down her veggie patty sandwich with sprouts and glanced over at the line. "Hey," she said. "Isn't that one of the Mason brothers with her?"

"Ed Mason," Joe said glumly. "He's the one who messed up my ankle."

Callie gave him a look that said she was being very patient with him. "Well, after all, Joe," she said, "wrestling is a pretty high-risk sport. You have to expect to get hurt now and then."

Joe barely heard. He was too busy watching Vanessa and Ed to remember to eat the half sandwich—roast beef on rye with mustard and pickles—in his hand.

Just when had Vanessa become so friendly with Ed? he wondered. And why? True, Ed did have all the smooth California show biz moves down, plus an easy smile and a great physique, but Vanessa was too smart to fall for that, wasn't she?

"Go easy on Joe," Frank told Callie. "People have been teasing him all morning about that limp."

"You've got to expect that, Joe," Callie retorted. "You've got too much hubris."

"Hubris?" Joe murmured, hardly paying attention.

"Sure," said Frank. "It means pride. Remember? In the old Greek tragedies, if a hero had too much hubris, the gods would strike him down."

Joe didn't hear. He was too busy concentrating on Vanessa as she bent her arm to show off her biceps. Ed felt it and acted very impressed. Then he said something that made Vanessa laugh. He laughed, too, and casually put his hand on her shoulder.

Joe felt as if they were laughing at him. "That musclehead!" he exclaimed. "There's really something I don't like about him."

Callie put down her sandwich and waved a finger at him. "Come on, Joe," she said. "Let it be. Green doesn't suit you."

"Green? You think I'm jealous?" he replied. "Not a chance."

"Well, you're certainly acting that way," Callie continued. "Don't be so possessive. Vanessa has a perfect right to talk and kid around with anyone she wants to."

"I know that," Joe said. He looked away from Ed and Vanessa and took a deliberate bite from his sandwich. It tasted like mustard-flavored dust between two sheets of cardboard.

"Oh, look," Callie said. "There's Ed's brother, Peter."

Joe raised his head to see a tall, thin guy with rumpled hair join Vanessa and Ed.

"You and Ed got off on the wrong foot, so to speak," Callie said, grinning at her own pun. "I don't know Ed, but he seems nice enough. As for his brother, I like him a lot."

"You do?" Frank said. "I didn't know you even knew him."

"Oh, sure," Callie said with a nod. "He sits next to me in physics. He's had some fascinating things to say about computers. What a brain that guy's got."

"You're not exactly sitting with a couple of dodos right now," Joe reminded her.

"Of course not, Joe," Callie said hastily, "but it's really a treat to talk to somebody with such intellectual range. He's totally committed to making a difference in life. He's thinking about the future of our species—space colonization, interstellar travel, stuff like that."

Frank laughed. "Callie, get real! Peter can't be that sharp. He's only eighteen. I'll bet his science fair robots are put together from kits."

Callie's face reddened, and she threw her napkin down. "What's got into you two today?" she exclaimed. "You're acting like a couple of five-year-olds."

As she pushed her chair back, she added, "I'm going to buy an apple—and enjoy it in a less toxic atmosphere."

She walked away with her chin in the air.

Frank started to get up to go after her, but Joe held him back. "She'll cool off."

"I guess so," Frank said as he watched Callie come out of the food line with an apple in her hand. Obviously not glancing in the direction of the Hardys' table, she walked over and sat with Vanessa and the two Mason brothers. "But maybe she's right. Maybe we *are* acting a little jealous."

"I'll tell you what," Joe replied. "Next time we see the Masons, we'll make a special point of being nice to them, okay?"

Frank nodded. He lifted his sandwich, then put it down without taking a bite. "I wouldn't mind getting a look at those robots, though."

At five o'clock that day Frank and Joe climbed the marble steps of the Bayport Museum, moving against the stream of people leaving as the place closed. Silence and the smell of floor wax hung in the air as they turned into the main hall, past a sign that said Closed for Display.

"Hold it right there, boys," said a man with short hair. He pulled a walkie-talkie from the pocket of his suit jacket and spoke into it as he continued to glower at Frank and Joe. "What's your business here?"

"We're Frank and Joe Hardy," Joe said. "Our dad is Fenton Hardy."

Since Joe couldn't go to wrestling practice and Callie had Latin Club, the two boys had decided to go downtown to see how their father was doing. Maybe, they reasoned, they could even help with some of his problems, which could take their minds off their problems.

"Mr. Hardy, huh?" said the man. "Stay right there, please, while I check this out."

Frank didn't like standing around in the hall while some hired muscle eyed him suspiciously. The guy in the suit and tie acted as if throwing Frank and Joe out on their noses would make his day.

It was a good five minutes before Fenton and the guard came back. Frank was relieved to see that his father was wearing a smile. He was more relaxed and rested than Frank had seen him since he took on the museum job.

"Boys, meet George Dawson," Fenton said. "He's one of the extra security men we've brought on board for the exhibition."

"The place looks different from the last time I was here," Frank remarked.

"You bet," Dawson replied. "Mr. Abrahamson has laid out a bundle to give it a real spit-polish. He's really going to put Bayport on the cultural map."

He turned and walked away.

"Sweet guy," Joe said, making a face. "Where did you find him?"

Fenton shrugged. "I didn't. He's on loan from the security force of a shopping center that Abrahamson owns."

"Abrahamson?" Frank asked. "Who's he?"

"He's a big real estate developer who put up the money to refurbish the museum and bring the Botrovian crown jewels here," Fenton explained. "He also financed the new alarm system."

"The one that doesn't work, you mean," Joe said. "Or that works too well."

"Actually, I think it's all right now," Fenton said with a smile. "We haven't had a single problem all day. Whatever the bug was, it seems to have cleared up. Since you're here, why don't you take a look at the exhibit? It's really something special, and once it opens, the crowds will

19

be so thick you won't be able to get near the display cases.''

Frank answered for both of them. "Thanks, Dad. That's a great idea.''

As they walked down the hall, Fenton asked, "Joe, how's that ankle of yours?''

"It's better today,'' Joe replied.

They walked past a pair of uniformed guards, who nodded to Fenton. "The museum doesn't usually have so many guards, does it?'' Frank asked.

Fenton shook his head. "Nope. This is a very special exhibit. If anything happened to any of these jewels, it would create an international incident. That's why the board of directors asked me to step in.''

"Being around all this culture makes me hungry,'' Joe remarked. He pulled a candy bar from his pocket and bit into it while listening to his father explain the new security system.

"It's focused mostly on the special exhibit area, of course,'' Fenton was saying. "We're about to go through one of the new sets of steel doors that shut at the first alarm and isolate the area.''

"Wow,'' Frank said. "I bet those cost a lot of money.''

"It all did,'' his father replied. "And that's just the beginning. Come on. I'll show you around. Oh—Joe?'' he added. "Would you please get rid of that candy bar wrapper? We don't want litter in here."

Joe glanced around but didn't see any wastebaskets. "Where, Dad?" he asked.

Fenton gave him an amused smile and pointed. Nearby, against the wall, was a three-foot-tall cylinder made of what looked like brushed stainless steel. The irregular patterns of raised designs that covered it made it look like something from a science-fiction movie. The top surface was almost flat, with only a slight depression in the center.

"Er—what do I do?" Joe asked.

"Put the candy wrapper on top, and watch," his father replied.

Joe did as he was told. The moment the paper touched the top surface, a circular panel slid open. The wrapper dropped through the opening, and the panel closed again.

"That's some gizmo," Frank said. "I noticed a couple just like it in the lobby, but I had no idea what they were. How are people going to know to put trash in them?"

"Fortunately, that's not my problem," Fenton said. "I think they're really odd. Still, they add a certain something to the place, as well as taking care of the trash."

He led them into a large room with no windows. Most of the room was dimly lit, but spotlights mounted on the ceiling shot beams of brilliant light into the display cases. Along the walls were more of those automatic wastebaskets.

Joe let out a low whistle that Frank echoed. Inside the cases were the most astonishing pieces of jewelry Joe had ever seen. Huge diamonds flashed like captured lightning, within intricately worked settings of gleaming gold. Bloodred rubies and dark green emeralds gave off mysterious glints, and pearls the size of pigeon eggs glistened with a luster that seemed to come from somewhere deep beneath their surfaces.

In the central case was the show's prize, a gold crown and scepter worked with dozens of jewel-studded animals, flowers, and people in medieval costume.

Frank had trouble taking it all in. Finally he said, "The gems and gold must be worth a fortune by themselves. But I know it's a lot more than that, isn't it?"

His father nodded, his face softening for a moment. "Yes," he said. "These are important works of art, created by the finest European artisans of their day. They're irreplaceable. It's a wonder that the Botrovians were able to hang on to them during the days when they were part of the Soviet Union—but that's another story. We just want to be sure to hang on to them *now*."

As Frank and Joe looked at the exhibits, their

father explained some of the features of the new alarm system. Frank had to admit he was impressed. The entire space was crisscrossed by infrared and laser beams. An interruption of any of the beams set off an alarm. Motion detectors and weight-sensitive panels were set into the floor, and there were hidden steel doors that could seal off the room.

"And, of course, each of the most important individual exhibits are separately protected as well," Fenton concluded. "I don't know what more we could have done. Now that the system seems to be working, I feel much more upbeat about the opening. The next time these alarms ring, I'll *know* it's a thief."

Fenton peered around the room, then added, "Everything seems to be under control here. What do you say we head home for dinner?"

Frank had wandered over to take a closer look at the doorway. The steel panels on either side were set into the walls so skillfully that he would not have noticed them if his father hadn't pointed them out earlier. He reached out to feel the cool, smooth edge of one of them.

Without warning a horn blared deafeningly. From the corners of the room, floodlights blazed into life.

Frank whirled around. His father's face showed sheer disbelief. Then, as he glanced in

23

Frank's direction, his expression changed abruptly to terror.

"Frank, the doors!" he shouted. "You'll be crushed!"

Frank looked over his shoulder as the two giant steel doors, like the jaws of some hungry beast, thundered toward him.

Chapter

3

FRANK THREW HIMSELF into a backward roll and hit the marble floor, just as the doors slammed together with an echoing crash.

"Frank! Are you all right?" Fenton cried. He rushed over to help Frank to his feet.

"I'm fine, Dad," Frank replied. This was not quite the truth. His hip hurt where it had slammed to the floor, and he felt pretty shaken up. Those doors had almost killed him. "What happened?"

"I don't know," Fenton answered, "but I'm going to find out. I'm also going to make sure they install a safety device so those doors don't close on a visitor."

When the doors slid back, four guards came

rushing in. "What is it, Mr. Hardy?" one of them asked. "Don't tell me it's another false alarm!"

"It looks that way, Tom," Fenton replied. "But do a thorough check of the premises anyway."

As the guards set about their work, Fenton said, "I'll be right back. I want to check the central console."

He returned a few minutes later, shaking his head gloomily. "Nothing," he said. "Absolutely no sign of tampering, no sign of an intruder. Nothing."

More to himself than to them, he added, "The only time I've come across anything as loony as this was fifteen years ago. But there's no way . . ." He fell silent, lost in thought.

"What was that, Dad?" Joe asked.

Fenton shook himself out of his daydreaming. "Nothing," he replied. "I'm afraid you're going to have to tell your mother and aunt that I'll be working late again tonight."

"That's okay, Dad. No harm done," Frank replied. "I guess we'd better—"

"Hardy!" a voice boomed. "Will you please tell me what on earth is going on here? Who are these kids?"

Frank turned. The man in the doorway looked like an NFL linebacker who had stopped working out and decided to eat instead. The jacket of his expensive suit strained at the shoulders and waist. The three men with him were of ordinary size, but next to him they looked even smaller.

"Terrific," Fenton muttered under his breath. "He *would* show up now."

"Is that the guy you were telling us about? The one who's sponsoring the exhibition?" Frank asked quietly.

Before Fenton could answer, the man in the doorway said, "I'm sponsoring this show, Hardy, and that means my name's attached to it. If anything goes wrong, it'll reflect badly on *me*. I don't need to tell you that that would make me very unhappy. And if you're the one who's responsible, I promise you, you'll be even more unhappy and for a whole lot longer. Now, what's the story here?"

"Another false alarm, Mr. Abrahamson," Fenton said in a taut voice. "But it's under control."

"I should hope so," Abrahamson barked. "I'm paying a fortune for this security system and for your services. When the board voted to hire you, they all told me you're the best. They'd better be right."

"I'll let you judge for yourself, when we've finished our work," Fenton replied. Frank and Joe noticed the two telltale angry red spots on his cheeks, but his voice remained steady and

27

level. "Oh, Mr. Abrahamson—let me introduce my two sons, Frank and Joe."

Frank would have liked to snub the overbearing businessman, but that would have embarrassed his father. He said, "How do you do?" and held out his hand. Next to him, Joe did the same.

"Hunh," Abrahamson said, eyeing them. He didn't seem to notice their outstretched hands. Reaching into his coat pocket, he pulled out a cigar and stuffed it in his mouth, then produced a gold lighter and clicked it.

As the end of the cigar began to glow, one of the men with Abrahamson said, "Er—I'm sorry, Mr. Abrahamson, but the museum has a strict no smoking rule."

Abrahamson drew in a mouthful of smoke, then blew it out toward the ceiling. "It's after hours, Dartry," he said, "and I'm on the board of this place, as well as being its most important contributor. A little cigar smoke won't hurt anything."

He turned back to Fenton. "I want a report on this on my desk tomorrow morning, Hardy—I don't care if it is Saturday. But most of all I want you to take care that this doesn't happen again. The exhibition is opening Tuesday night, no matter what."

Without another word, he strode out of the room, the other three flanking him.

28

"Whoo!" Joe said. "That guy doesn't think much of himself, does he?"

"Why are you working for such a toad, Dad?" asked Frank.

Fenton Hardy sighed. "I'm not. I'm working for the museum. But he's right about one thing—without his support, this exhibition and the re-vamping of the museum wouldn't have happened. So I guess it's natural for him to act as if he's in charge. Well, I'd better get back to work," he concluded.

"Is there anything we can do to help, Dad?" Frank asked.

"Certainly," Fenton replied. "You can go home now and try to smooth things over with your mom and aunt Gertrude. Tell them I'll be home soon, and that I'm doing just fine."

He didn't look as fine as he was trying to sound.

After dinner Frank and Joe went into their father's study and office.

"I don't like doing this," Frank said as he crossed the room to stop by the file cabinets.

"I know I don't," Joe replied, joining him. "But Dad's not here for us to ask permission, and we've got to do something to help. You saw the way he looked this afternoon. Haunted. He'd ask us to help if his pride weren't stopping him. So we have to do something." He started scanning the labels on the file drawers. "Are you sure he said fifteen years ago?"

"That's right," Frank said. "So it should be here in the file cabinets. He hasn't computerized these old files." He tugged one of the drawers open.

Fenton Hardy's files were neat and organized in green hanging folders. Each was labeled but only with a number.

"How do we know what to look for?" Joe demanded.

"We don't," Frank admitted. "But it's got to be some sort of theft from an exhibition or museum, right?"

Joe nodded. "That makes sense. Let's get to it."

They split up the files and sat down at the desk to pore over them. After half an hour Frank sat back and said, "That's it. Unless it wasn't really fifteen years ago, there's only one possibility—the Hastings Collection theft."

He retrieved the file, and together they scanned the neatly typed pages.

"Hmm," said Joe. "This seems to be exactly what we're looking for."

Frank nodded. "Dad was the security consultant to the collection and helped the owners install an alarm system to protect a very valuable jewelry exhibition," he said, summarizing the case aloud. "But someone managed to pull off a heist anyway."

"Who?" Joe asked. "And how?"

Frank smiled grimly. "Apparently the thief somehow set off a whole string of false alarms, until the officials of the collection decided to turn off the new system and rely on an older, less efficient set of alarms. Meanwhile, the thief had hidden himself above the ceiling tiles of the men's room. Night came, he crept out, got around the old alarm system, and escaped with the jewels."

"Pretty slick," Joe commented. "How did Dad manage to catch him?"

"He didn't," Frank replied. "The case was never solved."

Joe stared at him. "Never solved? That doesn't sound like Dad."

"I know, but maybe that's why he's so spooked by what's going on—because it reminds him of an old failure. But there's more. I found this slip of paper tucked into the file. It's dated three years later."

He began to read aloud.

New Haven museum theft case just solved, shows similarities to Hastings case, suggesting that the perp, Richard Courtland, was responsible for both jobs. No evidence against him in Hastings, and not much chance of finding any at this time, but at least he'll be out of circulation for a long time.

Joe whistled. "Richard Courtland?" he said. "I've heard Dad talk about him as the only really smart thief he ever met."

"I wonder . . ." Frank said. "If Courtland was caught twelve years ago, he must be out of prison by now."

"Right," Joe said eagerly. "But wait—once all those false alarms began here in Bayport, Dad must have started searching for some dude hiding in the bathroom. If anyone's there, Dad would have found him by now."

"Maybe that's why he's so frustrated. He hasn't found anyone. We'd better put these files back and make sure they're all in order," Frank replied as they heard the sound of the garage door rising.

"Dad's home," Joe said. "Do we ask him about the Hastings Collection robbery?"

Frank hesitated, then said, "Not yet. Let's go up to our room and power up the computer. Maybe we can track down Mr. Courtland for him."

A few minutes later Frank was tapping on the keyboard of his computer, while Joe leaned on his shoulder and watched the monitor.

"What are we accessing?" Joe asked.

Frank said, "The NCIF—the National Crime Information Files. Dad's a charter subscriber."

"Do they go back fifteen years?" Joe asked.

"No," Frank said, shaking his head. "But we might find some recent jewel robberies with a similar MO, or a recent reference to Courtland's whereabouts and activities."

"Good idea," Joe said. Just then there was a tap on the door.

"Boys?" Laura Hardy called. "Your father's home. Why don't you come down and join us for some dessert?"

"Thanks, Mom," Joe called back. "We'll be right there. We're just finishing up something."

"Ha!" Frank suddenly said.

Joe asked, "Got something?"

Frank nodded excitedly. "Richard Courtland was released from prison three and a half years ago and immediately moved out of Connecticut. Guess where he's living now?" He dramatically tapped the lower-right corner of the screen.

Joe leaned over his shoulder to check where Frank was pointing. There, in bright white letters on the blue screen, was the word *Bayport*.

Chapter

4

"I'M SORRY, JOE," Aunt Gertrude said. "How did I neglect to give you a piece of pineapple upside-down cake?"

Joe grinned sheepishly. "Well, actually, Aunt Gertrude," he said, "you did give me a piece. I finished it already."

"Anyone would think you hadn't had dinner," Laura Hardy said with amused resignation.

"That was over an hour ago," Joe said indignantly. "A guy gets hungry."

"Let him be, Laura," Aunt Gertrude said. "I like to see a healthy appetite. I just wish Fenton had one. He didn't touch his spaghetti, and now he's ignoring dessert. Not only that, he's not listening to a word I say!"

Fenton looked up. "What's that?" he asked. "Sorry. I've got a lot on my mind. I think I've lost my touch. Maybe I should throw in my cards, retire, and write my memoir."

Laura shook her head. "You'll never do that, Fenton. It's just not in you."

"Don't worry, Dad," said Frank. "You'll come through this just fine. That's a promise."

His father gave him a weary smile. "I wish I could take your word for it, Frank. Right at this point, I don't see many bright spots, just big, dark clouds." He stood up and started for the front hall stairs.

"What do you boys have on for tonight?" Laura Fenton asked after her husband had gone.

Frank shrugged. "Callie and I usually catch a movie on Friday night," he said. "How about you, Joe?"

"I don't know," Joe replied. "Okay if Vanessa and I double with you?"

"Sure, why not?" Frank said.

Laura shook her head. "You two are always so sure of yourselves. Have you already made these dates?"

"Well, no, not exactly," Frank said. "But Callie knows we always go out on Fridays. She's just a couple of button pushes away." He strode over to the kitchen wall phone and dialed Callie's number while Joe started stacking the dessert dishes in the dishwasher.

His mother picked up the threads of their old conversation. "I don't know what I'm going to do about your father," she said. "I can't remember seeing him like this. Are you sure it's just a security problem, Joe?"

"Mom, you know Dad better than I do," Joe replied. "But I do know that he takes a lot of pride in the job he does, and this one's not going well. Of course he's upset."

Laura shook her head. "Between him and you boys, I don't know who I worry about more. Joe, please be more careful when you wrestle. I have enough to worry about."

She broke off as Frank turned back to them from the phone. He had a puzzled expression on his face.

"I just talked to Callie's mom," he reported. "She says Callie's gone out!"

"Hey, don't worry, Frank," Joe said. "I'll just call up Vanessa, and you can tag along with us."

"Don't bother," Frank replied. "According to Mrs. Shaw, it was Vanessa who came by and got Callie—along with Bill, Chet, Biff, and Tony. Not to mention Ed and Peter Mason."

"The traitors!" Joe said.

"Well, well," their mother said lightly. "That works out very nicely. You two can heal your wounded male egos by helping me pick up the house."

Joe looked at Frank, and Frank looked at Joe. They both sighed. It had been that kind of week.

Saturday was a beautiful, clear winter day. The sky was a flawless blue, and the air had a snap that made you take deep breaths and stand taller. A perfect day for a hike, in fact, Joe thought wistfully. He rolled down the window of the van and took in a couple of lungfuls of air, then rolled it back up again.

"I'm glad I'm not going," he said suddenly.

Frank was driving and glanced quickly over, before turning his attention back to the road. "Uh-huh," he said, in a neutral voice.

"No, I mean it," Joe insisted. "I've got much more important things to do than go on some silly school hike."

"Granted," said Frank. "Helping Dad is important, but did you ever hear the story about the fox and the sour grapes?"

Joe scowled at him, but Frank was busy driving and didn't notice. To distract himself, Joe picked up the sheaf of notes he and Frank had compiled from the NCIF and a half dozen other data bases.

"Courtland, Richard," he read. "234 Benton Drive. Released on parole from Conn. State Prison 3½ yrs ago (time off, good behavior). Current position: Vice-Pres, Research, Intech Inc."

Joe glanced up. "How does an ex-con, a former jewel thief, land an important job with a big corporation, just a few months after he finishes doing time?" he demanded.

"You know the answer to that," Frank replied. "The guy's apparently something of an electronics genius. And second, one of those articles we traced down about Intech casually mentioned that Courtland's cousin is the CEO."

Joe nodded. Intech had been in the Bayport news a lot over the past few months. An international corporation and a major producer of state-of-the art computer hardware, it was now in the process of relocating both its manufacturing base and its executive offices to Bayport. As the local papers kept mentioning, it was terrific economic news for the town.

"The whole thing sounds fishy to me," said Joe.

"Joe the cynic," said Frank. "Look, there may be something fishy, true. But you have to remember, Richard Courtland has every right to be here."

"What?" Joe exclaimed. "We both know he only moved here to get his revenge on Dad by pulling off the jewel robbery of the century."

Frank made an exasperated noise. "Come off it," he said. "He moved to Bayport because the company he works for moved to Bayport."

"Ha!" Joe replied. "A company that his

cousin directs. He probably talked him into the move just so he could have an excuse for coming here himself.''

Frank concentrated on his driving. There was no point in talking to Joe when his mind was made up.

A few minutes later Frank pulled the van over to the side of the road and stopped. ''That must be the place,'' he said.

Across the road, in the center of a spacious, tree-studded lawn with a wooden fence surrounding it, was a large, two-story house, white with green shutters. At the side of the house was a garage. Joe took a pair of binoculars from the glove compartment and studied the layout.

''What now?'' Joe asked. ''Do we go knock on the door and ask if he wants to buy magazine subscriptions?''

Frank gave a short laugh. ''No, of course not. We sit tight until he leaves the house; then we follow him.''

''Funny thing,'' Joe said. ''That's a really big house. Courtland must make a lot of money at Intech. What could tempt someone who's made that much to go back to crime?''

''Maybe to show that he's still as clever as he used to be,'' Frank suggested. ''And, anyway, don't forget we're talking about tens of millions of dollars in jewels.''

"Well, I just hope we catch him trying something," Joe growled. "I could use a little action today."

"Just be careful you don't try any kickboxing moves with that sprained foot."

"Ankle, Frank, ankle. Besides, it isn't sprained. In fact, it feels better already." Joe lifted his foot and wiggled it.

"Enough clowning," Frank said. "There he is."

Joe raised the binoculars and said, "Yeah, that's got to be him. Distinguished-looking guy, I must say. Gray hair, sheepskin coat . . ."

One of the garage doors went up, and the man went inside. A few moments later a gleaming European sports sedan backed out and started down the driveway, while the garage door automatically shut itself.

Frank leaned forward and switched on the engine. "Here we go," he said, a note of excitement in his voice.

Half an hour later he and Joe were sitting in the van, parked outside a bank.

"What do you think, Joe?" said Frank. "Are we going to see Courtland come running out with money bags in one hand and a blazing pistol in the other?"

"Very funny, Frank," said Joe. "So far, he's stopped at the drugstore, a hardware store, a dry cleaners, and the supermarket. This guy is acting so normal that it would make me suspect he was up to something, even if I didn't already suspect him."

Joe drummed his fingers on the dashboard of the van. "And as I sit here, wasting my time," he continued, "my girl is off walking arm in arm with some overdeveloped geek. What a week— and last night was the pits. How could they do that to us?"

Frank cleared his throat and said, "You know, Joe, Mom had a point. It's not as if we had actually made dates with Callie and Vanessa. And it wasn't like they went out with just the Masons. They were part of a whole group. What were they supposed to do? Stay home just in case we happened to call?"

"But how could they go out with the bozo brothers when they could have gone out with us?" Joe demanded. "I don't understand."

"Joe, let's face it," Frank said. "Whether we like it or not, Ed and Peter have impressed a lot of people and made a lot of friends since they came to Bayport High. They're interesting, different—"

There was a light tap on Frank's window. Frank whipped his head around and was shocked to see a tall man with gray hair, dark brown eyes, and a long, sharp nose, wearing a sheepskin coat. It was Richard Courtland.

Frank rolled down the window.

"I know who you are," Courtland growled. "You're Fenton Hardy's brats. Well, here's a little present for you."

He reached inside his coat. An instant later he was pointing a gun straight at Frank's face.

Chapter
5

COURTLAND'S FINGER TIGHTENED on the trigger of the gun. Frank was trapped and helpless, but even more, he was furious at himself. How could he have allowed a guy he was following to sneak up on him like that?

He let out a gasp, as a stream of icy water hit his forehead and started to trickle down his cheek.

"Gotcha," Courtland said, then gave a chilly laugh. "Did you really think I wouldn't spot you following me? When I noticed these water pistols in the drugstore, I decided to let my punishment fit your crime."

He held up the black plastic water gun for Frank to inspect, then tucked it into his coat again. "Which one are you?" he continued. "Frank, or Joe? Frank, I'd guess. You look older."

"You seem to know a lot about us," Frank muttered.

Courtland raised one eyebrow. "Of course," he said. I read newspapers. I have a small collection of clippings of your exploits, as well as your father's. Though I must say," he added sadly, "Fenton Hardy would not be proud of your surveillance techniques this morning. Definitely third-rate. Now, if you'll excuse me, I have a lot to do today."

Joe was still angry about the fright Courtland had given them, and the anger could be heard in his voice. "Such as what?" he demanded. "Setting off false alarms?"

"False alarms?" Surprise played over his face. "Oh, I see. Well, you mustn't pay attention to your father's ridiculous suspicions about me. I'm a respectable, upstanding citizen—" His face hardened. "And don't you forget it."

"We were just wondering if you'd forgotten," Joe said roughly. "I've heard that once larceny gets in your blood, it never goes away. You planning any new escapades?"

"Sorry about Joe, sir," Frank said apologetically. "You can't blame him for wondering about your moving to Bayport, just before Dad

44

took on the job of protecting the crown jewels of Botrovia.''

Courtland's jaw dropped. "You're here about the crown jewels of Botrovia? Yes, I guess they *would* be a feather in my cap. Perhaps I should get out my cat burglar outfit again!" He paused to laugh at the expressions on Frank's and Joe's faces. "No, I don't think I will. I'm happy with the peaceful life of an ordinary man."

"I find that hard to believe," Joe said sarcastically.

Courtland's demeanor became icy. "Do you? Well, be that as it may, as a new resident of this lovely city, I would hate to have to file a harassment complaint against you two. I know Chief Collig socially, and I've heard that he is none too happy about you and your amateur detecting. A complaint from me might be just what he needs to bring you down. Or worse yet, I might even call your father. When was the last time he grounded you?"

"We're sorry if we bothered you, Mr. Courtland," Frank said earnestly. "Joe's got a hot head and a big mouth sometimes." Frank's attempt to appease Courtland wasn't wasted on Joe.

"No harm done." The smile returned to Courtland's face, but his eyes were as cold as ever. "I'll be on my way now. And to save you gas,

45

I'll tell you that I'm going straight home to make popcorn and watch a basketball game.''

He walked confidently back to his car.

"Well, he certainly made chumps of us," Frank said.

"You know?" Joe replied, his eyes half open and his voice smoldering with fury. "That guy bothers me!''

"Oh?" Frank said sarcastically. "I'd never have known."

For Frank and Joe the best cure for the late-afternoon blahs was a large mushroom-and-pepperoni pie at Mr. Pizza. At three-thirty, forty-five minutes after their encounter with Courtland, they were digging into one.

"I think there's only one thing for us to do," Frank said, deftly tucking a strand of mozzarella back onto his slice.

Joe took a bite of pizza, then said, "Oh? What's that?''

"Talk to Dad," Frank replied. "Tell him what we know. Compare notes."

Joe nodded. "Yeah. At the very least we've got to let him know that Courtland's in town."

"Hey! How are you guys doing?" Tony Prito brushed flour off his hands and sat down at Frank and Joe's table. "Where were you last night? Hiding out or something?"

"We were busy on a new case," Joe said,

46

then added, "Were you part of the Mason pack last night?"

"Oh, yeah. A whole bunch of us went out to dinner and then to the Billiards Room. Boy, Peter and Ed sure know how to play pool. Did you know that Callie and Vanessa were there?"

"Well, our case comes first," Joe said gruffly. "I guess Vanessa must have been pretty bored, huh?"

Tony laughed. "I hate to tell you, but she had a terrific time. The only one who laughed more at Ed Mason's jokes was Callie. And that Peter—not only was he making these incredible bank shots, but all the scientific stuff he was spouting, you'd think he was a college graduate. Callie seemed to be—" He abruptly stopped when he realized what he'd said in front of Frank.

Joe looked at Frank. Frank looked at Joe. They both looked down at their pizza.

Suddenly they weren't hungry.

"Uh, Tony," Frank said. "I think we're going to need a doggie bag."

At the museum they hunted up their father and presented him with the small pizza box.

"Pizza?" he said quizzically. "Thanks, boys. That was thoughtful. I'll get to it later. Right now, I have to wrap up these tests."

Fenton was hunched over a computer monitor. As each new screen came up, he touched his fingertip to various squares, then waited to see the results. He paused to explain, "The system has a wide array of self-diagnostics. Basically, what I'm doing now is asking it to test each of the different sensors individually, then by twos, threes, fours, and so on. We may be dealing with some weird interaction among different devices."

Frank looked at Joe, and Joe gave him back a you-tell-him look.

Frank took a deep breath and said, "Uh, Dad? Listen, we've been really concerned about you. So we decided to lend a hand."

"Did you? That's nice." Fenton continued to tap at the screen.

"Yeah, and we think we're onto something," Joe said. "We know about the Richard Courtland case, the museum theft fifteen years ago. And guess what we found out? Richard Courtland is living right here, in Bayport!"

Fenton hit a switch, sighed, and spun around in his seat to face his sons. "Boys, do you think I don't know that?"

Joe was surprised, but Frank had already considered the possibility. After all, Courtland was his father's old foe. "You didn't say anything about him," Frank said.

"He was my problem, not yours," Fenton replied.

"We were just trying to help," Joe insisted.

"I know, and I appreciate it." Fenton paused, then added, "It occurred to me that Richard Courtland was the obvious suspect for all our false alarms. We had coffee when he first moved to town, so it was easy for me to go to his house and have a little talk."

Joe was aghast. "You had coffee with him?"

"Sure. Why not? He's an interesting man, and he doesn't seem to hold a grudge. He's got a very good job now and is enjoying himself here. He's not in Bayport because of me—I can assure you of that. I tailed him for a day or so, and he's clean as a whistle. No, tempting as he may be, he doesn't seem to have anything to do with the problems here at the museum."

"So we're off base, suspecting him of setting the alarms?" Frank asked.

Fenton hesitated. "I didn't say that. Richard Courtland has a wily, unpredictable mind. He may be planning something. I'm keeping my eye on him, just in case, but so far I haven't seen anything that makes me think he's after the jewels."

"He knows you're suspicious, though?" Joe asked.

"Oh, yes." Fenton chuckled. "He even offered to come down and take a look at my alarms, to help out. Naturally, I refused."

Frank, deciding to come totally clean, told the

49

whole story—including their encounter with Courtland that morning.

"No reason to harass the man," Fenton said, amused. "I already have." He went back to testing his system. "Please tell your mother I'm going to make a definite effort to be home in time for dinner—but if I don't make it, tell her I have pizza."

"Can't we stay and help you?" Frank asked.

"Go on home, boys. There's really nothing you can do here."

"You know, if I had a tail, it would be between my legs," Joe said as he and Frank left the museum. He glanced up. Thick, dark clouds were moving in from the west, and the temperature was dropping. There was the promise of snow or cold rain.

"Well, I guess we should just swallow our pride and see what's going on with Callie and Vanessa tonight," Frank replied as they walked down the steps and started into the parking lot that was connected to the loading area at the back. "We've just—" The alarm inside the museum went off just then, interrupting him.

"Frank! Watch it!"

Out of the twilight darkness a green van came speeding from the parking lot and swerved toward Frank. Joe grabbed his arm and yanked him out of danger.

The van took a right out of the lot and peeled down the street, squealing through a red light.

Behind them, Frank could hear the alarm continue its warning shriek.

"Do you think whoever's inside that van had anything to do with the alarm going off?" Joe asked. "Come on, let's follow them."

Before Frank could reply, Joe had leapt into the driver's seat of their van. Frank scrambled in after him. Moments later they were speeding out of the lot in the wake of the green van.

"I bet they got off this street and made the first turn," Joe said. "I'm going to give it a try. Right or left, You choose." Frank pointed left.

Joe took the turn too fast and sped down the narrow street, which dead-ended at the intersection of another major thoroughfare.

"There, a couple of blocks ahead!" Joe turned right and tromped on the accelerator. The powerful engine roared, and the van shot ahead.

Frank leaned forward against his seat belt, straining to catch any details of their quarry.

"Can you see who's driving?" Joe demanded as the green van passed under a streetlight.

Frank shook his head. "Not a thing. We're still too far back."

"If I can just come even with him—" Joe passed a slow-moving car, and the driver of the car honked angrily.

Without warning a siren wailed behind them.

Frank checked his side-view mirror and saw a patrol car pursuing them, its red lights strobing against the darkness.

"Er, Joe," he said. "It's the cops."

Joe jammed on his brakes and pulled over to the side of the road. Knowing he'd been going too fast, he reached toward the glove compartment for the registration.

A voice boomed out beside him. "Get those hands on the wheel, fast!"

Frank risked a glance at the man. A scared-looking uniformed officer was standing outside the driver-side window, his hand on his revolver, ready to draw and use it.

Chapter

6

JOE CAREFULLY PUT his hands on the wheel, in plain sight.

The officer said, "Okay, get out of the car, slowly—"

"Hey, Fred, calm down," said another voice. "This is Frank and Joe Hardy's van—they're okay."

Joe gave an audible sigh of relief when he heard the voice of Officer Con Riley, the boys' closest ally in the Bayport Police Department.

"Well, now," Riley said as he walked up to Frank's window. "Suppose you explain why your brother was driving so recklessly?"

Joe was watching as Fred got out his book to write him a ticket.

"I was chasing a crook in a dark green van," Joe protested.

"Aren't you always?" said Officer Riley. "And what might these crooks have done?"

They nearly ran us down a couple of minutes ago. Beyond that, we're not positive," Frank admitted.

"Now, listen, Frank," Officer Riley said. "Civilians are not to chase criminals. That's *our* job."

Frank spoke quickly. "Oh, I know that, Con. I keep telling Joe, but he can't get it through his head."

"What!" Joe said. "Why—"

Frank gave him an elbow in the ribs and continued, "What if, instead of giving Joe a ticket, you took us downtown to have a little talk with Chief Collig? Maybe that would straighten him out."

Officer Riley rubbed his jaw. "Hmm—the chief is in now, and he looked like he needed to tear a strip off someone. Better Joe than someone on the force."

He looked over at his partner and said, "Scrub the ticket, Fred. We're going to give the driver a dose of stronger medicine."

As he talked, Chief Collig's red face seemed to swell up like a balloon being inflated.

"And if I ever hear about either of you speeding again while you're playing detective, I promise you that your driver's licenses are going into the deep freeze!" With that, the chief pointed at the door and the boys retreated through it. Outside, they were greeted by a smiling Con Riley.

"So, did you boys promise to stay out of trouble," he asked, his smile broadening into a grin. When Joe opened his mouth to protest, Con held up a finger as if in warning. "Frank," Riley said, "you didn't fool me. Tell me why you really wanted to come to the station."

Joe chimed in, "Yeah, why did we want to come down here? I didn't need the chief to chew me out."

"And you didn't need a ticket, either," Frank said with a grin. Then he became serious. "It's the van, the one that went speeding past us just after the alarm went off at the museum. The driver might be involved."

On cue Joe said, "I memorized the license number."

Riley thoughtfully drummed his fingers on the desk for a moment. "Since no crime has been committed, there's no reason for us to investigate. I guess there's no harm in checking this out. So, Joe, what's that plate number?"

Con entered the number into the computer on his desk and waited a short while, then said, "Okay, it's registered to a Bayport address, and it's a van, all right. Are you sure it was green?"

"Of course," Frank replied. "It nearly flattened me."

"Huh," Riley said. "It's listed as blue here. Somebody at Motor Vehicles must have hit the wrong key. Anyway, here's the owner's name."

The Hardys left the station and headed for their van. After Joe hopped in, he turned to Frank. "I'm totally baffled—that van is registered to Vanessa's mom, Andrea Bender. I've never seen it at their house, and you know how much time I spend there. *Did* spend there, at least," he added gloomily.

Andrea Bender owned a successful computer animation company and was one of the last people anyone would suspect of being a jewel thief. Still, it was the only lead they had.

Riley had wanted to know whose name they were expecting to hear. When they told him their suspect was Richard Courtland, he was outraged. As far as Riley was concerned, Courtland was a new and important member of the community and a friend of the chief's, not someone to be subjected to Frank and Joe's unwelcome attentions.

Vanessa and her mother lived just outside Bayport, in a big old farmhouse. Out back was a barn that housed Andrea's high-tech animation studio. It had burned down the year before but was completely rebuilt now. When the boys called to ask about the van, Vanessa invited them over.

By the time they reached the Bender place, the barn was dark. Lights shone in the ground floor windows of the house, though. As the Hardys pulled into the driveway, they saw half a dozen cars.

Frank recognized most of them. They belonged to his and Joe's friends. "What is this, Homecoming Weekend?" he asked.

"I don't know," Joe replied. "But I don't see a green van."

Frank pulled up behind Chet Morton's battered station wagon and parked, then he and Joe went around to the back door and knocked.

Mrs. Bender opened the door. She was wearing her usual work clothes, a gray sweatshirt and baggy jeans. "Hi, Joe. Hi, Frank," she said. "Come on in. Glad you could make it. We seem to be having a party tonight."

The kitchen smelled of fresh popcorn and woodsmoke. From the living room music with a heavy beat pounded out.

"Vanessa told me about your leg, Joe," Andrea continued. "How's it doing?"

"It's my ankle," Joe replied. "It's feeling better, thanks."

"By the way, Andrea," Frank said, "while we've got you alone . . ." He quickly told her

57

about the mysterious green van registered to her.

"So that's what happened," Andrea said mysteriously when he finished. "You've seen my minivan, which is blue. Well, last night, somebody stole the license plates off it. I was furious because getting new plates is a real pain. Obviously the thief put my plates on his car."

"Where was your minivan parked when the plates were stolen?" Frank asked.

"That's just it. You'd think something like that would happen on one of my trips into New York City. But no—someone stole them right here while I was out to dinner with some of Vanessa's friends. I came back and they went on to play pool."

Frank continued, "Do you happen to know a man named Richard Courtland?"

"Sorry, never heard of him," Andrea replied, slowly shaking her head.

"Was anything other than the plates stolen?" asked Frank.

"Not a thing."

"Well, hi there, you two!" Vanessa breezed into the room. Her eyes brightened when she saw Joe. "Where have you been? I tried to call you."

"We've been working," Joe said. "So, how did the hike go?"

"It was terrific," Vanessa said. "Come and

tell us how you're feeling. Ed says he figures what you really need is some vitamin E and magnesium supplements to help the healing process. He feels really bad about your leg, Joe. You ought to give yourself a chance to find out what a great guy he is.''

''I've got a pretty good idea what kind of guy he is already,'' Joe replied. ''But I do want to have a little talk with him.''

''Well, come on in,'' Vanessa said. ''Biff brought over some hot new CDs, and the hike left everyone really pumped.''

Frank and Joe followed Vanessa through the kitchen door and into the living room. The furniture had been pushed back against the walls, leaving room in the middle for half a dozen dancers. Over near the fireplace, another group was standing and talking. Just behind them was a table of refreshments.

''Hey, try these,'' Chet Morton called when he saw Frank and Joe. ''The Masons brought over some absolutely unbelievable veggies and health dip.''

''Hi, Chet,'' Frank responded. ''You went on the hike?''

''You bet! Hungry work, let me tell you! It's a good thing Ed brought along some trail mix and granola squares,'' he replied.

Vanessa laughed. ''I think he exercised his appetite more than his legs.''

"Chet did just fine," Ed said, raising a bottle of mineral water in a toast to him.

Callie came over to say, "Frank, glad you could make it."

Frank smiled, trying to disguise his lack of enthusiasm. "I hear you had a good time last night."

"Oh, we did. The Masons have brought lots of West Coast culture to Bayport." She motioned over her shoulder to the tall guy close behind her. "You know Peter Mason, don't you, Frank?"

"We've seen each other around. And of course I've heard a lot about him."

As they shook hands, Peter said, "Frank Hardy. Of course." He didn't bother to explain what he meant. His eyes shone with an intimidating amount of intelligence. "After talking with Callie, I feel that I know you."

"Were you on the hike, too?" Frank asked curiously as Ed and Chet drifted away.

"Oh, no. Like you, I was busy with other matters," Peter said with a sly glint. "My science project—homework. My schoolwork doesn't leave me much time for extracurricular activities, I'm afraid."

"My project is about ready to go," Frank said, and smiled tightly. "I've heard about those robots of yours. I'd love to see them if they're ready to show yet."

Peter smiled coolly. "Oh, you will, Frank. Count on it."

"Frank, Peter claims he never dances, so I've been showing him how. You don't mind if we try one more, do you?" Callie went on tiptoes to give Frank a quick peck on the cheek.

"Well, actually," Frank said, "I was hoping Peter and I could talk about his robots a little more."

Peter grinned. "What can I say, Frank? She's turned me into a dancing machine." Peter and Callie moved into the center of the room as Vanessa went to check on the food.

"Those Masons *are* too good to be true. It just came together for me," Joe said to Frank. "They're a couple of junior-grade crooks."

Joe ticked off the points on his fingers for his brother. "The Masons were here last night before you went to dinner, right? And I'm willing to bet that one of them was left alone for a while at some point." He glared across the room at Ed Mason.

"A couple of hours ago we were almost run down by a van with Vanessa's mom's license plates—the ones somebody stole, just last night. Peter didn't go on the hike, and I'll bet Ed got back early. These yo-yos make no secret of the fact that they don't like us. The only thing we don't know yet is if they have a green van. So we just have to pin that down.

"Can't our friends see what they are? How can everybody be so dense?" He had moved even closer to Frank to be heard over the music, but he realized that Vanessa had come up behind him and was listening to him. He yelled at Vanessa, "Have they fooled you all?" just as the music ended.

A shocked silence fell over the room. Ed Mason detached himself from Chet and moved back to Vanessa's side, smiling easily.

"Is he bothering you, ma'am?" Ed asked. He fell into the pose of an old-fashioned boxer, then aimed a couple of mock swipes at Joe's jaw.

Joe ducked as everyone joined in the fun and laughed. When Ed fanned the air with a left, Joe automatically brought up his fists. It looked as if he were joining the mock fight.

"Another round," someone called.

"Joe, you're awful," Vanessa cried. She spun around and stalked away.

"Vanessa," Joe called, turning after her. "Wait, we have to—"

At that moment a rock-hard fist landed solidly on Joe's jaw.

Chapter

7

JOE HARDY STAGGERED backward from the blow and hit the edge of the snack table, hard. It caught him sharply in the small of his back, and he fell to the floor while bowls of dip and plates of cut-up vegetables spilled over and around him.

"Hey, I'm really sorry, Joe," he heard Ed say. "You bobbed when I expected you to weave." Joe heard the nasty edge to Ed's voice. Hurt and angry, he stood up and swung out at the guy who'd hit him.

Ed dodged easily and thrust out a leg. Joe tripped over it and fell back against the table again, scattering everything that was left.

"Hey, come on, dude, chill," Ed said. "I was just playing around. My apologies."

Everyone stared as Joe rose and brushed salsa and chili-cheese dip off his shirt.

Vanessa stepped up very close to Joe. He searched her eyes for a sign of sympathy, but they revealed none. "Joe," she said very quietly, "you have done your best to ruin my party. It'll be a long time before I forget this."

"It's all my fault," Ed said, stepping between Joe and Vanessa.

"No. No, it's not, Ed," Vanessa replied. "It's Joe's fault, and before he leaves he's going to apologize, to you and all of us."

Joe felt his jaw drop. "Apologize?" he shouted. "No way. He hit me!"

"If that's your attitude, I want you out of here," Vanessa replied.

Joe couldn't decide if he felt more like a victim or a fool. Whichever, he didn't feel good.

"Well, boys," Vanessa's mom said from the kitchen doorway, "I see you've had one of your little adventures—and all over my living room floor, too. I'm sorry, but I think it's time for you to leave."

Frank hated shoveling snow with a passion.

There he was, anyway, pushing a shovel under the fresh blanket of white stuff that had fallen during the night.

"Well, Joe," he said. "Nothing like an exciting Saturday, followed by an even more exciting Sunday morning."

Joe glumly swept the porch steps. "Tell me about it," he groused. "Ed made such a fool of me—and right in front of all my friends!"

"That's okay," Frank said as cheerfully as he could manage. "Since they're our friends they'll forgive and put up with us.

"Are you going to call Vanessa and apologize?" Frank asked.

Frustration crossed Joe's face. "I tried last night. I tried this morning. No answer. My guess is that she's just not ready to speak to me yet."

"Don't take it so hard," Frank said. "Think of all the fun you'll have making up."

Joe picked up his brother's snow shovel to relieve him for a minute. "And to think I used to *like* snow!"

Frank grinned. "So let's go over this again, Joe. Why do you suspect the Masons of setting the false alarms at the museum?"

"Well, motive and opportunity," Joe said. "It would have been very easy for Ed or Peter to pull the plates on Friday. Whoever stole them had to know where to find them, right? I don't think it's coincidence that the plates came off one van and onto another. The thieves must have hoped that any officer who called in the plate number would make the same assumption

65

Con Riley made, that the color listed in the DMV file was a mistake."

Frank nodded. "Okay, I'm with you so far. But who's to say the thieves didn't simply cruise around, searching for a parked van?"

"Frank, that green van swerved toward you. I saw it," Joe said grimly. "Why? I say it's because the driver recognized you and wanted either to scare you or hurt you. But who'd want to do that? The same guys who've been sniping at us every chance they get—the Mason brothers. They obviously know Dad's working on security at the museum, so if they can foul it up, they make all of us appear even more foolish. So there's motive, and opportunity I already covered."

"You're forgetting a little matter called evidence," Frank pointed out. "We don't even know if the Masons own a van, whether it's green, blue, or polka dot. And you can't pretend to be an impartial investigator, Joe. Face it, you want Ed to turn out to be a crook, because of his interest in Vanessa."

"Well, Frank, you don't exactly seem pleased about Callie gushing over Peter's exquisite brain," Joe snarled.

Frank took a deep breath. "Joe, I told you, I trust your instincts, but logic tells me that this is a stretch."

"You're right. I'm sorry." Joe shrugged. "So

I'm human. Sue me." He sighed. "Just who do you think the Mason brothers are?"

"I've seen their type before," Frank replied. "They're new in town, and they're determined to make their mark, fast. And let's face it, they probably see us as their main competition. But it's a long stretch from trying to steal somebody's friends to trying to steal the crown jewels of Botrovia. I still think that Richard Courtland's our best suspect."

"Or someone else we don't even know about," Joe suggested.

Frank replied thoughtfully, "That's a good possibility. In any case, I think we should keep investigating."

"So what's our next step?" Joe asked.

"The green van—what make do you think it was?"

"I'm eighty percent sure it was a new Silhouette. I haven't seen many of them around."

"I agree," Frank said. "Now, I wonder if we can find a way to use Dad's data base to access car registrations? There's no way Con Riley will help us twice."

They hurried to finish up their wet and chilly task, then went inside to boot up the computer.

"Funny," Joe said about fifteen minutes later. "I've been checking new telephone listings against last year's directory. As far as I can tell, there aren't any new Masons in Bayport."

Frank, hunched over the computer, barely heard his brother. "Maybe it's an unlisted number."

"Nope," Joe replied. "They'd still be listed but without an actual number."

"Maybe they don't really exist," Frank suggested. "Maybe they're aliens. Or ghosts. Anyway, if you want their phone number, ask them for it. Tell them you want to organize an Ed and Peter Fan Club."

"Am I getting on your nerves?" Joe asked.

"Sorry. This is tricky, that's all," Frank replied. "Hey, okay! I've managed to track down a file from City Hall of new car registrations broken down by make. Now, if I can just figure out how to specify the search criteria . . ."

"Terrific," Joe said. "While you're doing that, I'm going to try Vanessa again."

Finally someone at the Bender house answered.

Clearing his throat, Joe forced out, "Hi, Vanessa? It's Joe."

"Hello, Joe," Vanessa replied, her tone a few degrees cooler than the snow outside.

Joe swallowed, then said, "Look, Vanessa, I'm really sorry about what happened."

"I'm sure you are, Joe," she said. "And I imagine I'll forgive you—tomorrow. Maybe. But right now I'm still too mad to even talk to you. 'Bye." There was a click, then a dial tone.

"She hung up," Joe reported to Frank.

"Um? Oh, too bad. But look what I've got." Frank held up a printout, with the names and addresses of four owners of new Silhouette vans.

An hour later the boys had crossed off three of the names.

"Too bad that list didn't mention the color of the vans," Joe remarked. "It would have saved us a lot of trouble. Who's next?"

"Jane Smith," Frank read. "Sounds pretty suspicious, doesn't it? Here we go."

A few minutes later he pulled up in front of a house surrounded by a high fence with a hedge planted in front of it to hide it. As they got out onto the sidewalk, Joe glanced upward. The sky had turned gloomy and dark again; more snow was on the way. Joe reflected that detective work didn't always mean excitement and surprises and adventure. A lot of it was dull, routine, drudge work—like checking out the owners of Silhouette vans.

"Hmm. It doesn't look as if anybody's home," he remarked.

"Any sign of a Silhouette?" Frank replied.

Joe peered. "I can't see anything through that hedge."

"Yes, the place is pretty heavily protected," Frank said thoughtfully. "That is a little suspicious, isn't it? You have that survey question-naire ready, just in case?''

"Right here." Joe showed him the question-naire they'd prepared before leaving their house, asking Silhouette owners how satisfied they were with their new vans, then folded it and stuffed it inside his coat.

They walked over and opened the gate. The front yard was empty. Concrete walks led up to the front door and to the driveway. Joe went over to peek inside the glass windows of the garage.

Inside, he could see the dark form of a van, but the dust on the glass made it impossible to tell the color or even the make.

He rejoined Frank and reported, "There's a van in here. This must be the place."

They went up to the front door, and Frank rang the bell. Instead of hearing footsteps, how-ever, Joe heard a much less welcome sound.

From behind the house, a dog began to bark. A big dog. A moment later, another joined in. And the sounds were coming closer.

"Uh-oh," Joe said urgently. "Maybe we'd bet-ter get out of here."

Frank didn't seem to need any encourage-ment. He turned and sprinted for the front gate, Joe right behind him. Frank grabbed the latch, but nothing happened. "It's jammed," he shouted.

Joe peeked back over his shoulder, just in time to see two German shepherds come tearing straight at them.

"Over the fence!" Frank yelled. He grabbed one of the uprights and vaulted over the jagged top of the tall fence with a gymnast's grace.

Joe started to follow, but he had forgotten about his injured ankle. He couldn't jump high enough and fell right back into the yard. He tried again, and this time got a hand on the top, but then he felt something tug at his pants leg. He glanced down and stared into a pair of eyes filled with blood lust.

"Down, boy," he said, without much hope.

The dog's answer was to pull backward. Joe's grip on the fence began to slip, and just then the second dog jumped at him.

Chapter

8

JOE'S PANTS LEG RIPPED as he yelled, "Frank! Do something!" Frank frantically battered the gate.

From behind him, a woman's voice called, "Homer, Jethro! Heel!"

"You'll be okay, sonny," said their owner as the dogs gave one more tug for good measure, then released Joe's legs. "They just like to play."

Joe let himself down gingerly and turned to face the elderly dog owner as her German shepherds took up positions on either side of her.

"What can I do for you, young man?" she asked.

Frank finally managed to open the gate. He

stepped inside but held the gate open, just in case. "Ma'am," he said, "we're doing a survey, and we'd like to find out how you like your new van."

The dogs barked as if in answer. Joe flinched, then said, "Ah! I take it that means that Homer and Jethro like their new green van."

"Green? Sorry, my new van's red." With a smile, she added, "Now, you boys have a nice day."

The dogs howled in agreement.

Monday morning as the Hardys slogged through Bayport High School's slushy parking lot Joe told Frank, "I still say that green van we saw is registered in Bayport. But things may be looking up. Today Vanessa might forgive me. And we might have scared the thieves away."

Frank laughed. "I see you're getting your optimistic self-confidence back," he teased.

They headed for the auditorium, where early arrivals gathered to wait for the bell. As they walked in, Joe glanced around, and his heart sank. Just a few feet away were the Mason brothers, talking and laughing with Callie and Vanessa.

"Take it easy, Joe," Frank muttered. "Just remember, everybody's friends with everybody."

"Sure, right," Joe muttered in reply.

"Well, if it isn't the life of the party," Ed said with more than a touch of malice.

Joe kept smiling. "Listen, I want to apologize to you guys. To you, Ed, for acting like a jerk. And to you, Vanessa, for spoiling your party."

"Spoiling it?" Peter exclaimed. "Not at all. You were the high point of the evening!"

When Vanessa raised her eyes to Joe's, she had only a trace of forgiveness in them. Joe glanced at Ed and Peter and noticed that they both looked exhausted. Peter stifled a yawn, and Ed had trouble keeping his eyes open. He wondered what they'd been up to on Sunday.

"We were just talking about Peter's robots," Callie said. "I can't wait for you guys to see them. Peter, why don't you tell Joe and Frank a little about what you're doing?"

Peter seemed reluctant. "I don't know, Callie. I hope to patent some parts of the project. That's why Mr. Wilson's letting me use that empty storeroom to work in, so that I can keep everything private."

Callie laughed, her eyes bright with enthusiasm. "Oh, come on, Peter. You can trust Joe and Frank."

Peter clearly could not contain himself and began to talk, his tiredness forgotten. "Robots aren't news anymore, but there are so many new developments that no one's applied to robotics—fiber optics, ultra-large-scale integrated circuits, powerful reduced instruction set computer processors, lasers. What I'm doing is putting all these together to make something where the whole is more than the sum of the parts."

"Sounds great," Joe commented. "But what are these robots of yours good for?"

Callie answered. "Tons of things—they could deal with hazardous wastes, radioactivity, space."

"Imagine," Peter said. "Robots could be sent into space to repair satellites, conduct sensitive experiments, even explore distant planets, all under the guidance of a remote ground station."

"That's exciting," Frank said, "but isn't radio control iffy from long distances."

Peter nodded. "It is, ordinarily. But I've greatly increased reliability and incorporated artificial intelligence concepts in the software."

"Your computers think for themselves?" Frank asked.

"Only in a limited sense," Peter said.

Frank nodded. "Fascinating, Peter. It sounds like you're onto something. I'd love to see your machines in action."

"Peter wouldn't feel too comfortable about that, not yet," Ed said. He didn't appear to be particularly comfortable himself.

"I'll make a deal with you, Frank," Peter said. "I'll give you a preview before the science fair next month. But only if you'll do the same for me."

"Fair enough," Frank replied.

"Frank, listen to me," Joe said. "Those guys have a van—a green Silhouette van."

The three o'clock bell had just rung, and they were standing at Joe's locker.

"Really?" Frank replied. "You've seen it?"

Joe shook his head. "Well, no. But I was talking to Phil Cohen last period, and he said it was a really souped-up number."

Frank thought for a moment, then said, "The Masons didn't have a van at Vanessa's."

"No, they were there in a four-by-four," he said. "But maybe they have two cars."

"There's one way to tell," Frank said. "Let's go take a look around the parking lot."

As they walked outside, Joe thought about his day. Things had gone better with Vanessa, a lot better. They even had a date for the next Friday night. The only sour note was that the Masons took every chance to put in sly digs at him and Frank.

Joe and Frank began to cruise the parking lot. A few acquaintances waved, but nobody lingered. It was too cold and slushy for that.

"No sign of a green van," Frank said.

Joe pointed. "Yeah, but there go the Masons."

Peter and Ed seemed to be arguing about something and didn't notice Frank and Joe as they walked across the lot to get into a four-by-four with a ragtop.

"Satisfied?" Frank asked Joe.

"Not necessarily," Joe replied. "They may have left the van at home. And, wouldn't you like to know exactly where home is?"

"Good thinking," Frank said.

They waited while the Masons backed out of their slot, then followed at a discreet distance. As soon as the four-by-four reached the street, it took off quickly.

"Are they in a hurry or what," Frank said.

Frank followed the other vehicle through back alleys and across shopping center parking lots. When the Masons hit the interstate and sped up to well over the limit, Frank said in disgust, "They're playing games with us, Joe. I won't play."

As Frank lifted his foot from the accelerator, the Masons' car suddenly cut across three lanes of traffic and swerved onto an exit. Frank watched in helpless anger as the boys escaped.

"Let's go by the museum," he said after a moment, trying to control his temper. "I think it's time we told Dad what we know and suspect. He may lecture us about sticking our noses in his case, but it's worth it if it gets us a lead."

Twenty minutes later they were at a table in

77

the museum cafeteria. It was a different Fenton Hardy sitting across from them, stirring his coffee.

"Things are great," he said, leaning back. "They couldn't be better."

"You're not worried anymore, Dad?" Joe asked.

"No. I believe I've found out what was wrong with the alarms. I had an expert in today who took one look, made a few adjustments, and promised that our problems are over. So far, all the tests are positive. Apparently, a faulty microchip may have been responsible."

"Oh," Frank said, aware that he was not doing a good job of hiding his doubt and disappointment.

Fenton glanced at him, then at Joe. "But tell me, what's on your minds?"

Joe said, "We wanted to tell you that we hadn't gotten very far in working out who might have tripped the alarms."

"Probably because nobody tripped them," their dad replied. "So you can drop your investigation and put your energies into other things. Which reminds me, Frank. How's your science project going?"

"Okay, I guess," Frank said.

Fenton frowned. "You sound like you've run into problems. Have you?"

Joe broke in. "It's just that he thinks he's

going to be totally outclassed by Peter Mason's Super 'Bots.''

"Super 'Bots?" Fenton repeated, raising one eyebrow. "What are they?"

"Robots, Dad," Frank replied. "This new guy's project uses some special kind of remote-controlled robots. He's quite a brain. As for winning the science fair, it's not that important to me. My minilab will be really useful to Joe and me, and that's what counts."

"Remote-controlled robots, huh? I'd like to see them," Fenton said, a curious cast to his expression. "And there's nothing wrong with a little competition, Frank, or with coming in second, as long as you've given it your best shot."

"I'm not the only one who's got competition," Frank said. "Peter's brother, Ed, was the one who hurt Joe's ankle in wrestling last Thursday."

Joe reddened. "I told you, it was because he cheated!"

"Whoa, fella," Fenton said, holding up a hand. "It sounds like a spirited rivalry."

"Yeah. I guess so," Frank said. "Until now, we even suspected them of being your culprits."

"Yes, Dawson?" Fenton said to the grim man with the crew cut who had just dashed up to the table.

"Phone call for you, Mr. Hardy," the security man said.

"Thanks." Fenton drained his coffee cup and pushed his chair back. "Well, boys, I really enjoyed the break. When you get home, tell your mother I'll definitely be home for dinner tonight, but I've got a couple of things to attend to first."

Before he walked off, he added, "It sounds to me as if these Mason boys are having a good time, mostly at your expense. Don't let them get to you. Your best weapon is a good sense of humor."

Frank and Joe made their way out of the museum. As they were walking down the front steps, Joe suddenly snapped his fingers. "State of the art!" he exclaimed.

Frank looked at him. "What about it?"

"That alarm system is supposed to be state of the art, and so are Peter's robots. Maybe there's a link. Maybe that's why Dad seemed so interested when we were telling him about the robots."

"You think the Masons could be using robots to trigger those alarms?" Frank asked.

Joe nodded. "Could be, and maybe they're about to pull off a robbery by remote control."

Frank was thoughtful for a moment. Then he said, "I can't see it. Dad said the problem had been solved by a systems analyst. Anyway, how would anyone smuggle robots into the museum? And even if they could, don't you think the secu-

rity force would notice a bunch of robots scooting around?''

"Good point," Joe said. "But I still have a
hunch, only a hunch, there's something to it.''

Frank frowned. "It's possible, I guess—if Dad
hadn't said the problem was solved. But the only
way to find out for sure would be to study Peter's robots, and that won't be easy.''

"Who needs easy?" Joe demanded, grinning.
"What are we waiting for?"

During the week Bayport High School stayed
open after hours for extracurricular activities
and a few evening classes. Getting into the building was no problem. Getting into the science
labs would be a different story.

As he and Frank walked down one deserted
hall after another, Joe muttered, "I've got a
credit card for slipping the lock.''

"Sorry, these doors only take cash," Frank
quipped. "But don't worry. I happen to have a
fine set of lock picks in my pocket.''

Stopping at a door, Frank glanced in both di-
rections, then brought out a ring of bent flexible
steel rods. He tried one, then another, until finally he heard a faint click.

"That's about the only good aspect of the
school budget crunch," he said. "Cheap locks.''

He pushed the door open and slipped inside
with Joe right behind him. Then he closed the

door and both of them started groping for the light switch.

Suddenly an alarm began clanging. Lights flashed, strobelike, from different corners of the room. By the unstable light, Frank saw several machines rolling rapidly toward him and Joe. The metal robots were each about three feet high, with an array of flashing sensors where their heads ought to be. Metal arms jutted out from the sides, with different tools at their ends. One was fitted with heavy hammers. Another raised something that looked like hedge clippers.

"Thief!" an electronic voice cried from each machine. *"Thief!"* The voices screeched so loudly that the windows rattled. *"Thief! Thief!"*

Chapter
9

THE ROBOTS SURROUNDED FRANK, waving tools at him. They were easy to dodge, but the howl of the siren and the repeated cries of *"Thief!"* were like the scraping of fingernails on a blackboard.

"Joe," Frank shouted above the racket. "Find the alarm and turn it off."

Joe was scrambling to find the control box when something hit him on the leg. One of the robots was whacking at him. The blows weren't hard, but did hurt.

Joe jumped away from the little machine and continued searching for the alarm box. At last he spotted it, attached to the wall opposite the door. He and Frank must have interrupted an infrared beam when they entered the room. Joe hurried over to throw the switch.

"Thief!" Another blow just missed his knee.

"Oh, shut up," Joe muttered. He turned and was about to give the contraption a swift kick in the microcircuit, when Frank rushed over and hit a switch on the robot's back. The lights on its head went out and it fell silent as had the other robots. Frank had made it around to all of them.

"Come on," Frank said, grabbing Joe's arm. "We've got to get out of here!"

They turned to leave the room but found themselves facing one of the custodians, the school secretary, and Mr. Wilson, the head science teacher.

"It's a good thing you two didn't damage anything. But I can't keep this quiet, you know. I'll have to tell Peter Mason, for one."

"Look, Mr. Wilson," Joe said. "We told the others that we had the wrong room, but we want to be straight with you. I think that Peter Mason and his brother, Ed, are planning to use these robots in a robbery—and I wanted to check out the robots."

Frank, clearly troubled by the whole business, could only nod. "It could be true, sir."

Mr. Wilson studied Frank and Joe thoughtfully, his bushy black eyebrows lowered with concern. "Look, I know you two mean well. And I know that you've made quite a reputation as detectives. Still, you have to realize how this looks. People will think that you were checking out Peter's science project because you were worried about the competition at the science fair."

"That's not true, Mr. Wilson. I'd like to win, sure, but I don't care enough about winning to cheat. You should know that about me."

The science teacher nodded. "Even so, people will talk. I'm not going to report you to the principal this time, Frank. But, please, don't let anything like this happen again."

As they walked outside to their van, Joe said, "One more goof-up. We must be setting a new record. I'm inclined to believe we're following the wrong scent."

"Not a chance," Frank replied. "While I was putting those gadgets away, I got a close look at them. I'm on your side now. I think it really is the Masons."

Joe shrugged. "Why?"

Frank let some of his excitement creep into his voice. "Several of the components had makers' labels on them. They all came from an outfit called Jax Robotics."

"So?" Joe said.

"When we were checking out Richard Courtland, I read a couple of articles about Intech, the company he works for. One of the articles mentioned that Intech has a subsidiary that focuses on robotics. Guess what it's called."

"Jax, of course," Joe ventured.

As they drove off, Joe said, "Let me get this straight. Are you trying to tie Richard Courtland to Peter's robots?"

"Maybe," Frank replied. "I don't know."

"But just because Jax Industries makes electronics parts, that doesn't mean Courtland or the Masons are involved," Joe objected. "Peter Mason could have simply bought the parts somewhere."

Frank said, "They're not something you pick up at your neighborhood hardware store, Joe. Some of the stuff there was so sophisticated that I think it's only sold to research firms. And don't you think it's too much of a coincidence that Richard Courtland works for the company that makes the parts Peter is using to build the robots that may be making our dad crazy?"

"You're right. We've got to check it out," Joe responded. "But when we do go let's remember that Intech is a high-tech outfit and bound to have pretty good security. I don't think those picks of yours will do the job."

"I agree," Frank replied. "That's why we're going to have to rely on stealth and guile—and a healthy dose of plain old good luck."

*　　*　　*

Intech occupied a long, low building along the front boundary of the Bayport Industrial Park. Frank steered the van over the tracks of a railroad siding and came to a stop near the main entrance. A few windows here and there were lit, but most of the building was dark as the night outside.

"What's our story going to be?" Joe asked softly.

"I don't know," Frank admitted. "Just follow my lead and keep your fingers crossed."

They got out and went to the double plate-glass doors. Frank pointed out one of the metal plaques attached to the doorjamb. Jax Robotics, it read, in dignified letters. He tried the door. It was locked.

"There's a night bell here," Joe said. He pressed it. A few moments later a middle-aged man in a guard's uniform appeared and unlocked the door. The nameplate on his left shirt pocket read Evans.

"Yes?" he asked. "What is it, boys?"

"Hi, we're here for the papers," Frank said. "For Mr. Courtland."

The guard was puzzled. "Mr. Courtland? Sorry, fellows, but he's left for the day. Try tomorrow."

"No, we know that, Mr. Evans," Frank said quickly. "He asked us to pick up the papers and bring them to him. Something about the Jax product lineup. He needs it tonight, for a presentation he's making. Didn't he call to let you know?"

Evans shook his head. "Nope, but I'm just the relief man. The regular man is on his dinner break. Maybe you'd better wait and talk to him."

"Mr. Courtland said it was urgent," Joe contributed. "He told us we'd find what he needs in the Jax showroom. Can't we just scoot in and get it? We won't disturb anything."

Evans rubbed his chin while he studied them. Frank did his best to look like a model of trustworthiness.

"Well—I guess it's okay," he finally said. "But you make sure you go straight there and come straight back. No wandering around."

"Thank you, sir," Frank said. "Er—where do we go?"

The guard pointed. "Left at the first corridor and about halfway down," he said. "You can't miss it. It's got Jax on the door in gold letters."

A few moments later Joe and Frank were looking in amazement at a showroom full of robot parts—the tiny but powerful electric motors, the complex steel and plastic skeletons, the sensors that were their eyes and ears, the incredibly complicated arrangements of gears and cables that moved them, and the almost jewellike arrangements that would be their hands. On the walls were pictures of machines that featured some of the components. One was deep underwater, cutting through the hull of a sunken ship. Another was apparently floating in space.

Frank took a camera from his coat pocket and began clicking pictures, while Joe wandered around the room and took a closer look at the devices on display.

After a few minutes Joe said, "Frank? We'd better get out of here. What if the regular guard gets back from dinner and finds out we were let in? He might call Courtland. He might even call the cops."

"I'm almost done," Frank replied. He, too, was starting to feel nervous. "There. Now— what are we going to take with us to show Evans? How about one of these brochures?"

He held up a thick catalog on heavy paper. The cover featured the photo of a Jax-equipped robot in space.

"Great," Joe said. "Let's go."

"Did you find what you needed?" Evans asked as he unlocked the front door for them.

Frank held up the brochure. "Yes, we did, thanks. Have a good night."

As they drove away, a compact car pulled into the company parking lot. The driver, a beefy guy in a guard's uniform, eyed them suspiciously as they went past.

"Oof, that was close," Joe said. "I hope Evans doesn't get in trouble because of us."

"I doubt if he'll even bother to mention our visit," Frank said. He glanced at the clock on the dashboard. "We'd better get home. Mom is probably wondering where we are. And after dinner, we can develop these pictures."

Laura Hardy rushed up the moment they walked into the house. "Frank, Joe," she said, looking utterly distraught. "I'm so glad you're home at last."

"What's wrong, Mom?" asked Frank.

"It's your father," she replied. "He hasn't come home, and I—I'm afraid something's happened to him."

"We saw him this afternoon," Joe said, patting her shoulder. "He was fine then. He probably had to work late again."

She shook her head violently. "No. He called to say he'd be home no later than six. When he didn't show up, I checked at the museum. They said he'd left. He should have been home hours ago."

"Still," Frank said, "you know how it is. Maybe he ran into somebody he had to talk to and he forgot to call. He'll probably turn into the driveway any minute now."

"I wish I could believe that," his mother said. "But I went out myself right after six, to run a

90

couple of errands. I just got back and was listening to a message on the answering machine.''

They followed her over to the telephone table in the front hall. She pressed the Playback button on the machine.

The message was in what sounded like a man's voice, but it had obviously been electronically distorted.

"Frank and Joe Hardy," the voice said. "Stay away from the Bayport Museum—or you'll never see your father alive again."

Chapter

10

"I WISH I KNEW what was happening," Laura Hardy said. "Anything would be better than all this waiting and uncertainty."

"I think Joe and I should go out looking for him," Frank said.

"No," his mother said sharply. "We'll all sit tight until we hear from the police—or the kidnappers." Just then the doorbell rang.

"That must be the police," Joe said.

Frank hurriedly got to his feet. "Maybe they've got news about Dad."

They hurried to the door, followed closely by their mother. Frank got there first and tugged it open. A uniformed police lieutenant stood there, with two other officers right behind him.

"Mrs. Hardy? I'm Lieutenant Malecki. May I come in?"

"Please do," Laura Hardy said. "Is—is there any news?"

Malecki shook his head. "No, ma'am. I'm afraid not."

"Stay away from the Bayport Museum. . . ."

Frank rewound the tape. Lieutenant Malecki had taken the original but not before Frank made a copy for himself. He played it again. He'd lost count of how many times he'd heard it.

"This proves we're close and on the right track," Joe said. "It must be the Masons."

Frank gave an absentminded nod.

"And the electronic distortion of the voice," Joe continued. "They obviously have access to sophisticated electronics."

He smacked a fist into his palm. "I'm telling you, Frank, they're connected to Jax somehow. They have to be. Did you see some of the prices in that brochure? There's a fortune tied up in those robots we saw at school. Where does a kid like Peter come up with that kind of money?"

"Good point," Frank replied. "On the other hand, Richard Courtland has even easier access to Jax electronics, and lots of experience as well. We really can't cross him off our list. I wish I didn't have the nagging feeling that we're overlooking something that should be horribly obvious.''

Joe paced the room, then stopped and threw up his arms. "I know—what if Peter and Ed are working for Courtland?''

Frank shook his head. "Why? He has the skills and equipment to do the job himself. And you're assuming that Ed and Peter do, too. So why do they need one another?''

Suddenly he snapped his fingers, then reached for the telephone.

"Who are you calling?" Joe asked.

Frank held up a hand for silence, then said into the phone, "Bayport Museum? Yes, I know the museum's closed. This is Frank Hardy speaking, Fenton Hardy's son. Thanks, I appreciate your concern. Listen, is a man named Dawson still on the premises? One of the special security detail? Oh. Can you give me his number?''

Frank scribbled it down, then pressed the disconnect button and dialed again. After introducing himself, he said, "Do you remember this afternoon, coming over and telling Dad that he had a phone call? How long was that before he left the museum, do you know? I see. And do you happen to remember who the call was from?''

When Frank hung up, he had an odd expression on his face.

"What is it?" Joe demanded.

94

"Shortly after that phone call, Dad left the museum unexpectedly," Frank said slowly. "It's possible that he had an appointment with the caller—one he never returned from."

"Well, come on, spill it," Joe said, his voice rising. "Who was it? Courtland? One of the Mason kids?"

Frank shook his head. "No. It was Mr. Abrahamson. The guy who's putting up the money for the show. We may have been looking at this case from the wrong angle all along."

"Run that by me again," Joe said a few minutes later. "Why would Abrahamson want to kidnap Dad?"

"To keep Dad—or us—from ruining his plan to steal the crown jewels," Frank replied. "How did the jewels get to Bayport in the first place? Abrahamson brought them here, that's how. Why? So he could steal them. And because of the money he's put up, he has the inside track on the new alarm system. He's even got some of his own people on the security force."

Joe frowned. "Yeah, but what about all that money he's put in? It doesn't make sense."

Frank sighed impatiently. "I don't know how much he's contributed," he admitted. "But I know one thing. It's bound to be peanuts, compared to the millions the jewels are worth."

"But what does he know about electronics?"

Joe continued. "What about the robots that are setting off the false alarms?"

"What robots?" Frank demanded. "Joe, you're the only one who's decided the robots are being used. Dad told us he found the problem in the system. The only robots we know anything about are the ones in the science rooms at Bayport High. And with the kind of inside help he's got, Abrahamson wouldn't need any electronic gadgetry to set off the false alarms. His men on the staff could do it themselves, easily."

"Boy, this opens up a whole new load of suspects," Joe said. "What do we do now?"

Frank reached for the phone again. "I'm going to call Richard Courtland," he said. "After all, he and Dad are supposed to be on friendly terms these days. If he's not the guy we're after, maybe he can help. And if he acts suspicious, maybe it'll give us more to work on."

Frank dialed Information and gave Courtland's name and address.

After a short pause the operator asked, "Which number would you like, sir?"

Frank raised his eyebrows. "I didn't know there was more than one," he said.

"Oh, yes, sir," the operator said. "At that address, we have a listing for Richard Courtland. And we also have a separate listing for the children's line."

Frank copied both numbers, thanked her, and

hung up. Then he told Joe what he had just learned.

"Children?" Joe said, puzzled. "There wasn't anything in the files about Courtland having children. But the information in those files goes back a long time. Maybe he's had them since he got out of prison."

"It's possible," Frank replied. "But he's only been out for three years or so. That means they can't be more than two or two and a half. I know times are changing, but that's still a little young to have their own phone line."

"That means he must have had them before he was sent to prison, twelve years ago," Joe said. "So they're in their teens now. Funny—I don't know any kids named Courtland at Bayport High. Do you?"

Frank shook his head. "No. We'd certainly have heard about them if they transferred into school in December, when Courtland moved here."

He fell silent. Then he and Joe stared at each other with widening eyes.

Joe finally broke the silence. "It can't be," he said.

"Of course it can," Frank replied. "We were looking for some kind of connection between Courtland and the Mason boys. I think we just found it. Ed and Peter must be Richard Courtland's sons."

"Impossible," Joe said.

"Why? Run it down," Frank said. He counted his points on his fingers. "Courtland moved here in December. Ed and Peter Mason moved here from California in December. And there are no new listings for anyone named Mason in Bayport. We checked. Add to that the fact that Courtland's a brilliant, unscrupulous crook, and that Peter's brilliant and Ed's unscrupulous. It adds up."

"Evidence," Joe protested. "We need evidence. What about birth certificates?"

"We can't call the Bureau of Vital Statistics at this time of night," Frank retorted. "Besides, we don't know where they were born. But there's an easier way to check. Either Callie or Vanessa should have the Masons' phone number. If it matches the one for the Courtland children's line . . ."

No one was home at Vanessa's. Callie's phone didn't answer, either.

"Out with dear Ed and Peter?" Joe said through clenched teeth.

Frank scowled. "On a Monday night? I don't know about Vanessa, but Callie stays in on Mondays. I guess she could be at the library, though."

"Or could be in trouble," Joe replied.

"Okay, don't panic," Frank told him.

Joe went back to pacing the room. "Why not?

98

Someone's kidnapped our father, and now maybe our girlfriends, to put pressure on us to drop the case. What if we don't? Who's next, then? Mom and Aunt Gertrude?''

Frank spoke calmly. ''I already asked Lieutenant Malecki to put a police watch on the house. And both Mom and Aunt Gertrude know not to go out. Now, let's just think this out, Joe. We've got a lot of circumstantial evidence—one phone call, a buggy alarm system, a missing father, two suspicious guys at school who may prove to be the sons of an old adversary of Dad's—''

''Not to mention high-tech robots and so many millions of dollars in jewels that even the sponsor might be drooling over them,'' finished Joe.

''That's a lot, but it still doesn't add up. There's got to be something that will clue us in to what's happening.''

Joe snapped his fingers. ''At Courtland's house. Remember when his garage door opened and he backed out? I got a quick look inside. That garage is deep, and it looked as if there was a workshop in there.''

Frank nodded. ''That's right. We figured at the time it was just an ordinary home workshop. But if Peter and Ed Mason live there, that workshop could hold exactly what we're looking for.''

''And if nothing else, we should question Courtland to find out if the Masons—and maybe Dad—are there,'' Joe said.

"There's something else in here somewhere, I just know it," Frank murmured. "Something that struck me as wrong."

"No use in sitting around here, trying to remember what it was. Let's get moving," Joe said.

Frank had to agree. Still, something nagged at the back of his mind, even as they headed out to their van.

It was late and the streets were wet and slippery with freezing rain. Frank drove carefully.

"Come on, Frank, move it," Joe said. "There's no telling what's happening at Courtland's. We might even be able to do something useful for a change."

Frank wasn't listening to Joe. His brain was working overtime. "What's the common denominator here?" he asked. "What is the one thing we know for sure?"

"Dad's alarm systems were fouling up," Joe said promptly. "And Dad's kidnapping proves that that wasn't an accident."

"Exactly," Frank said. "So something was causing the foul-ups. What? How? If we assume that the Masons and their dad were responsible, we can make a pretty good guess. We saw the answer to that tonight, at school."

"Robots!" Joe exclaimed. "Just like I've been saying."

"Exactly," Frank agreed. "If a robot can go into a damaged nuclear plant and retrieve radioactive rubble, it can certainly go into a glass case and retrieve a diamond and ruby necklace—or lots of them. And setting off a bunch of supersensitive alarms would be no problem at all.''

"But how do they get them through security?" Joe protested. "A robot is going to be a lot more conspicuous than a human being.''

The road curved at the top of a hill. Frank started to say, "I think the answer may be in that gar—'' when the steering wheel jammed. The speedometer needle had been hovering at forty-five. Now, as the van started down the slope, it began to creep up. Frank tried to move the steering wheel, to nudge the van back toward the center of the road, but it was as if a giant hand had seized the wheel.

"Hey, slow down," Joe said, alarmed.

"I'm trying, but we're sliding. I can't control the speed.'' Frank hit the brakes. They finally caught and worked, but too well. The high whine of the damp tires sliding along the freezing wet road filled the van. Slowly the back of the van began to come around—they were traveling sideways now, still sliding and going too fast. Through the windshield the two boys could see where they were headed—straight toward a thick, sturdy tree.

Chapter

11

FRANK GRABBED for the handle of the emergency brake as his right foot pumped the brakes. When they hit the gravel that ran along the edge of the road, he pulled the emergency brake hard, locking the rear wheels and spinning the van. Shoulders hunched, he waited for the crunch of the tree hitting the back fender. For one heart-stopping instant, Frank was sure they were going to roll over, but the resistance of the soil was enough to slow them down. Just short of the tree, the van spun to a stop.

Frank killed the engine and took a deep breath. "The steering went out," he said. "Just like that."

Joe nodded and reached into the glove compartment for their heavy-duty flashlight. "Pop the hood," he said.

Frank did so, then joined him at the front of the van.

"Well," Joe said, aiming the bright beam down at the steering box. "You see that square thing attached to the linkage? I don't think that's standard equipment."

"What is it?" Frank asked.

"I don't have the slightest idea," Joe replied. "But I'm willing to bet that's what caused our problem."

He went around to the back of the van and returned with the toolbox. While Frank held the light, he carefully detached the small box, then studied it curiously.

"When I have a little time, I'm going to figure out what it did," Joe promised.

"You don't see any Jax trademarks on it, do you?" Frank asked.

"I see we're thinking the same thing," Joe replied. "The Masons. But once again we have no proof. We're not going to get any prints off this gizmo. And what about Dad?"

"There's only one way to find out," Frank said grimly. "Get back in the van. If it'll run, we're going to pay Richard Courtland a little visit."

The Hardys hopped back into the van. Frank started the engine, put the van in gear, and drove off. After the removal of the box, the steering seemed to be cured.

When they arrived, the Courtland house was dark. Frank tried the front door. "Locked," he reported.

"Let's break in," Joe suggested. "For all we know, Dad's tied up in the cellar right now."

Frank shook his head. "Give me a break. This place is probably so rigged with alarms that if we sneeze too loudly, we'll have the One Hundred and First Airborne landing in the yard. We could try the civilized alternative, though." He reached over and pressed the doorbell.

"Good move, Frank," Joe said. "What'll you say? 'Oh, hello, Mr. Courtland. Did you or your sons happen to kidnap our father?' "

No one answered the door.

Joe said, "Let's check the garage." They stood on tiptoes to peer in the small windows set high in the garage door. By the light of Joe's flashlight, they saw that the garage was empty. As they had noticed before, the back had been made into a workshop, but a drop sheet now obscured most of it. Joe played the beam over the part they could see.

"Any robots?" asked Frank.

"Nope," Joe replied. "Some welding torches, though. And some kind of sheet metal and paint." He snorted. "Great. Maybe Ed's a sculptor, too. Vanessa would go nuts about that."

Joe clicked off his light. "I say we go in. We're smart. We can dope out the alarms."

"That will take time," Frank pointed out. "It does look more and more as though Ed and Peter are up to something. Something to do with Peter's robots. The exhibit opens tomorrow night. What if they're going to try the heist tonight?"

"So what's the plan, Frank?"

Frank bit his lip. "It's just the two of us—so if we split up we'll be twice as effective."

"What—you on foot?" Joe scoffed. "Or me?"

"No, no. We'll go back and get Mom's car," Frank explained. "You drive it over to the museum to check for anything suspicious. I'll take the van and cruise around, hunting for the Masons. The school, Intech . . . You can take the cellular phone from home and I'll use the car phone in the van. That way we can stay in contact."

Joe nodded. "Sounds good to me, but if nothing happens, then can we storm this place?"

Frank hesitated, then said, "We'll see, Joe. We'll see."

When Joe returned to the Bayport Museum, he found that many workers were still there. The revolving doors were locked, but the small door beside them was open.

The guard at the front desk raised his eyes from the bank of surveillance monitors and peered at the driver's license Joe gave him. After a moment, he said, "Oh yeah. Right. You're Fenton Hardy's kid."

"Yes, sir, that's me," Joe said. The guard's name tag said Michaels.

"Sorry about your father. The police came around to ask about him. Hope he's okay," Michaels said.

"Any problems with the security system for the jewels?" Joe continued.

"Don't talk to me about that thing," he replied. "It's been a pain from day one. But no problems tonight. It's a good thing because the custodial staff's been here polishing this whole place up for the opening tomorrow."

Joe cleared his throat. "Mr. Michaels, do you mind if we go back and take a look around before the show? With my dad out of touch like this, I'm pretty worried."

Michaels's head bobbed up and down. "I don't see why not. I'll have to call Stan to keep an eye on these monitors, though. Can you believe it? We've got a five-person security team tonight, as well as those fancy alarms."

"Great. Thanks. I'll just make a quick call and be right back." Joe took a few steps away from the desk, pulled out his cellular phone, and dialed Frank.

"Just cruising," Frank reported. "I took a lap around Intech, and now I'm headed for the school. No sign of the Masons so far."

"I'm checking on the jewels," Joe told him.

"No problem with the guards?"

"The man I'm dealing with knows Dad," Joe replied.

"Okay. Good luck. Talk to you soon." Frank disconnected.

Joe turned to see Michaels watching him, with a curious expression on his face.

"If you're done," the guard said, "I'll take you in there. You can see for yourself that those jewels haven't budged."

As they entered the dimly lit gallery, Michaels unwrapped a stick of gum and offered one to Joe.

"No, thanks," Joe said. He stared at the gleaming, priceless jewels, and could almost understand the urge to steal something so unique and beautiful.

"Everything seems to be okay," he told Michaels.

"You bet it is," Michaels replied. "No thief in his right mind is going to try to knock over this place, with all the security measures we've got." He crumpled up the gum wrapper and tossed it onto the top of the nearest modern trash receptacle. The top silently slid aside and swallowed the wrapper, then moved back into place.

Funny, Joe thought. He didn't remember seeing one of the containers there before. One of the janitors must have moved it, unless it had just been installed.

Frank Hardy drove on with a bitter taste of failure in his mouth.

This was a fool's mission, driving around on the off chance that he might spot his adversaries. The only excuse he had was that it was better than doing nothing.

He drove past the high school, then began to retrace his path to Courtland's house. A light ground fog was gathering, giving the street a dreamy look. Frank rolled down his window, hoping the cool night air might wake him up. It shocked him that he was losing his edge. He reached down and turned off the heater.

The headlights of an oncoming car made two tunnels of white in the mist. Behind them, the shape of the vehicle was indistinct. It was only when it was nearly level with Frank that he realized it was a van—a green van.

As it sped past, Frank killed his lights and swung his wheel, making a quick U-turn. He got into the right lane, and like a dark ghost, accelerated after his prey.

Up ahead, he could still make out the van's

rear lights in the mist. He turned on his lights and began trying to close up the distance between them. When he hit the top speed he felt comfortable with, he pulled out the car phone and called Joe.

"Yeah?" answered his brother. "Frank?"

"That's me," he replied. "I just spotted a green van heading east on Harrison. I'm not positive it's them, but it is heading in the direction of the museum. If it is them, they may have Dad."

Frank was about to add a warning when just ahead, out of the darkness and the mist, something was flung onto the road from the van. It looked like a sack with something in it. Something the size and shape of a human body.

Frank slammed on the brakes. The van skidded to a stop just short of the sack.

"Frank?" Joe said. "What's going on?"

"I'll call you right back." Frank dropped the handset and jumped out of the van. His teeth were chattering with dread and cold. The body in the sack—it could be his dad!

He hurried over, glancing at the shadowed trees on either side of the road. It was risky to be exposing himself, he knew, but his concern for his father outweighed any danger to himself. He tugged at the drawstring at the neck of the bag.

A burst of bitter white gas sprayed up into his

face from the neck of the bag. He gasped and felt himself choking, growing numb, falling. He could hear the van's engine idling. He could feel the pavement beneath him, smell the nearby trees.

Then darkness closed in on him.

Chapter

12

JOE DIALED the number of the car phone again. Still no answer. And no the-party-you-are-calling-is-away-from-the-vehicle message, either. Frank had left the phone turned on, but hadn't come back to the van. What had happened to him? And more urgent still, what should Joe do now?

He went to the men's room, ran some water in the sink, and splashed his face with it while he considered his options. Frank had told him to stay put, no matter what. Joe couldn't afford to go running off because if the jewels were stolen, he would have nothing to trade for his father. On the other hand, even if the Botrovian jewels were worth millions of dollars, his father and Frank were priceless. Joe knew what he had to do.

He hurried out of the men's room and into the front hall. Michaels was just settling down in front of his bank of monitors again.

"Mr. Michaels?" Joe said quickly. "Will you keep a really sharp eye on those jewels for me? I'm going off to find my brother. Can I have your number here?" He scribbled it on a slip of paper, then added, "If you don't hear from me in half an hour, I'm somewhere between here and Bayport High, probably on Harrison, and in very big trouble."

Michaels grinned. "Don't worry, son. I'll send in the marines."

Joe looked him straight in the eye. "The Bayport police will do fine. And I'm serious about that."

Michaels sobered. "You boys—what is it? You attract trouble like a magnet. Don't worry, though. I'll do just what you said."

"Thanks, Mr. Michaels. And remember. Keep an eye on those jewels!"

Joe raced out of the museum and jumped into the driver's seat of his mother's sedan. Joe was proud of his driving ability, and he would be putting it to the test now. As he turned onto Harrison, he thought of his father and Frank and he became very afraid.

If a police officer stopped him, then all the better. He could use the help. He could do without this mist, though, he thought as his mother's big sedan knifed through the dark and the fog. It was getting worse, as though the sky and the ground were trying to confound him.

Joe's mind ran over the facts in the case again. A couple of miles from the museum, that's what Frank had said.

Just past two miles, Joe saw something parked at the side of the road. It was difficult to make anything out in the fog, but when he got closer, there was no mistaking it.

It was the Hardys' van.

Joe pulled off the road and killed the engine. After yanking a flashlight from the glove compartment, he bounced it in his palm, feeling its comforting mass, then climbed out and shone it at the van. No one was in the driver's seat. He cautiously walked over, holding the flashlight more like a club than a lantern.

The van was empty, the door unlocked, the keys in the ignition.

There wasn't any sign of Frank. There was no sign of foul play, either. Something must have happened to him, something bad, but apparently it hadn't happened in the van.

Joe was trying to decide if he should put in a call to Lieutenant Malecki and tell him the whole story, when a car approached and slowed to a stop. Its powerful driving lights bored holes through the rolling mist.

Two men got out, slamming the doors behind

them. They seemed to be wearing long black coats and snap-brim hats. As they drew closer, Joe saw that one of the men was Mr. Abrahamson. His expression was grim. The other was Abrahamson's hired muscle, Dawson. In his right hand was a big, efficient-looking automatic.

Joe stood very still, his mind racing.

The men walked toward him. "Joe?" called Mr. Abrahamson in an ominous voice. "Joe Hardy?"

"That's right," Joe replied, trying to decide what to do next.

Was Abrahamson the culprit? Had he masterminded the whole thing? If so, he'd really gotten the drop on Joe. Was this how it had been for Frank, too?

"Thank heaven we found you!" Abrahamson exclaimed. "Ted, put that thing away. You know Joe Hardy."

Joe's tension eased as Dawson tucked his gun into a belt holster under his coat.

"How did you get here, Mr. Abrahamson?" Joe asked.

"I heard about your father's disappearance, and it just confirmed all my worst fears," Abrahamson replied. "I am not going to let any crooks spoil this exhibition. I've put too much of myself into making this show a success. Tonight I couldn't stop thinking about all of our problems. So, I picked up Ted Dawson and drove by the museum, just to make sure nothing was wrong. When the guard told me you'd just left and that you were worried about your brother as well as your father, Ted and I decided to find you."

Dawson ran an experienced eye over the scene. "What happened here?" he asked.

"I'm not sure," Joe told him. "I was talking to Frank on my cellular phone and he just disappeared. Now I really don't know what to do."

"Why don't we help you look?" Abrahamson suggested.

"Thanks, sir," Joe said. "I can use all the help I can get."

Abrahamson nodded. "Well, I'm glad you're okay, at least. I knew this exhibit might have problems, but I never imagined it would threaten people's lives." He reached into his pocket, pulled out a candy bar, and started to unwrap it.

Joe stared at him.

Abrahamson noticed and gave a self-conscious laugh. "It's a habit I've tried to break," he said. "Without much success. Would you like one, Joe?"

He produced a second candy bar and handed it to Joe.

When Joe stared at it, he felt as if he were watching facts click into place. The candy wrapper going into the cylindrical covered wastebasket . . . the painted sheet metal in the back of Richard Courtland's garage . . . and the robots, of course . . .

Joe stuck the candy bar into his pocket and announced, "I've got it!"

It was Abrahamson's turn to stare. "What? You know where Frank and your dad are?"

"Not yet," Joe replied quickly. "But I understand what the thieves are up to. I understand how they're planning to steal the crown jewels."

"How?" Dawson asked skeptically.

"Not now!" Joe pulled the cellular phone from his pocket and tapped out Michaels's phone number at the museum.

"What are you doing?" Abrahamson demanded. The phone rang.

"Come on, answer!" Joe looked at Abrahamson and said, "Robots. That's what's been messing up the security system."

Dawson gave him a contemptuous look. "Robots? Ridiculous. Don't you think our guards would have noticed a bunch of robots running around the place?"

"Not if they're disguised and controlled from a remote station. Or if they're preprogrammed."

"But how—"

The phone rang and rang. Finally a voice answered. "Look, I'm sorry. Things are crazy down here and I can't talk."

It was Michaels.

"This is Joe Hardy. Those trash cans are really robots. Knock them over, at once, then—"

He suddenly realized that what he was hearing in the background was the museum's alarms going off. There was a loud crash as Michaels must have dropped the receiver.

Joe turned to Abrahamson. "We have to get back to the museum, right away," he said.

From the outside, the museum appeared peaceful and calm.

Joe screeched the van to a halt by the front entrance and jumped out. Abrahamson pulled in behind him, and Dawson, driving Laura Hardy's car, finished up the caravan.

Not waiting for the others, Joe dashed up the steps to the front door. It was locked, of course. He rang the night bell, then pounded on the door. Jingling keys, Michaels hurried over to let him in.

"What's going on?" Joe demanded.

"Another false alarm," said Michaels. "We had to turn the whole system off. But we told the police everything's okay."

"It's *not* okay!" Joe shouted. "This is the final part of their plan. Let me in."

"Do it, Michaels," Dawson said, joining Joe at the door. Abrahamson was puffing up the steps behind him. "I'll take the responsibility."

Michaels stepped aside, and the three charged

117

in. Joe sprinted across the lobby, to the spot where one of the artistic, high-tech trash receptacles had stood.

It was gone.

"The jewels," he shouted. "They're stealing the jewels, right now!"

"Come on, Joe, calm down," Michaels said. "We checked on the jewels just a few minutes ago. Everything's fine. And anyway, we've got a man in there to keep an eye on everything."

Joe didn't waste time on further explanations. He dashed down the hall toward the gallery, then skidded to a halt in the doorway.

The lights were dim as always, but in the shadows, he could see the body of a security guard on the floor near the first of the display cases. Joe ran to the guard, who was breathing steadily, then abruptly froze. Deeper in the darkness, something was moving. Something about three feet high that gleamed like brushed stainless steel. Joe moved toward the fallen man.

The cylinder rolled forward, into the dim light. Moving, it didn't look at all like a trash receptacle. It looked like what it was—a stainless steel column. It moved toward Joe on a triangle of wheels that had popped out of the base, while Joe continued to the fallen guard. Three arms had emerged from the column's sleek outside. One appeared to carry a miniature television camera. The other two carried a variety of tools—and of course all it had to do was open its top to catch any jewels that it harvested. Above all, it did not look friendly.

Remembering his encounter with the robots at the high school, Joe made an instant decision to try to knock this one over. He crouched down, then launched himself into a jump kick. But he had forgotten about his injured ankle. It twisted under him, and he crumpled to his knees.

The robot rolled closer, then paused, as if it didn't know what to do. Joe quickly forced himself back onto his feet. From a concealed opening in the side of the robot, a stream of white gas sprayed straight at him.

Joe felt the gas envelop his face. It stung his eyes and burned his lungs. He held his breath and lunged for the robot, but once again his ankle made him unsteady, and he wobbled. He gasped, drawing in a lungful of the gas, and felt as if the walls were rushing in toward him.

Chapter

13

THROUGH THE FOG that was swallowing him and his thoughts, Joe heard people running. That welcome noise was followed by shouts and then coughs as others hit what was left of the clouds of gas. Finally someone grabbed him under the armpits and dragged him out of the cloud and into clear air. Suddenly he realized that again he could breathe fresh, cool air.

He gulped the air in hungrily. After a few moments he felt himself reviving. Shakily, he stood up and looked around. The guard who had been down on the floor was coming around, too.

"What is it?" Abrahamson demanded, grabbing Joe's shoulder. "What's the matter?"

Dawson answered for him even though he was

still coughing. "Gas," he said. "If the kid's right, what we've got here is a robbery in progress."

Joe, his vision clearing, looked down the hallway. A cloud of gas still hung in the air, and on the edge of it was one of the trash receptacles, lying on its side. He pointed to it. "That's what I meant," he announced. "Your high-tech trash cans are actually robots. And they're about to deliver the crown jewels to whoever made the robots."

Joe approached the fallen robot carefully and turned it over to reveal the cleverly recessed wheels, avoiding the still slowly moving arms. The top clattered to the floor, spilling a few scraps of paper to the floor. Joe tugged at the bottom of the trash compartment. It came out, exposing a tangle of wires and an integrated circuit board.

"And I bet that some of the components will be labeled Jax," Joe said.

Dawson drew his gun and held a handkerchief over his mouth. "We can deal with that later," he declared, and ran forward into the dissipating gas.

"I'll make sure the police are alerted," Abrahamson said, retreating toward the lobby.

Joe took a deep breath and followed Dawson. The gas was nearly all gone, but he could still feel it stinging his eyes. All the lights were on now, and he soon found Dawson standing in front of the main entrance to the special exhibits room, staring into it.

Joe ran up to him and then stopped.

No one was in the exhibit room now, but clearly someone had been. Shards of thick glass covered the floor, with a few stray pieces of priceless jewelry among them. An instant survey told Joe that almost half the Botrovian crown jewels were gone, including the scepter and the crown itself.

"Since we saw nothing as we came in from the front they must be heading out the back, through the service entrance," Joe said, pointing. "That's the only other exit. Everything else is barred at night."

"The service entrance is guarded," Michaels said. "We've got two men there."

"Not if they've been gassed, we don't," Dawson replied, sprinting in that direction.

Joe was about to follow, when he remembered the close brush he and Frank had had with the Masons' green van just outside the museum, on Saturday. The van had sped out of the loading area at the back of the museum into the parking lot, going the wrong way on a one-way drive. Joe had a strong hunch that that had been a rehearsal for this night's performance. If so, he was going to make a few unplanned changes in the script.

Moving as quickly as his ankle allowed, Joe hurried from the museum and clambered into his van. He had just started up the engine when he saw that he was a few seconds too late. A green van came roaring out of the parking lot and screamed around the curve of the museum access drive.

Instantly Joe cranked the wheel around and tromped on the gas. The van's powerful engine let out an angry roar, and he was on his way, close behind the escaping thieves. Closer, he hoped, to rescuing his father and his brother.

Joe had to use all his skill as a driver to keep the other vehicle in sight. Its driver must realize by now that he was being followed, and he tried one trick after another—screeching the wrong way down a one-way street, speeding abruptly onto and then just as suddenly off the interstate—but Joe stuck grimly to his tail, figuring that he was on his own because every cop in town had to be at the museum.

The green van raced down a stretch of wide streets lined with stores, then suddenly made an amazing turn into an alley.

Gritting his teeth, Joe yanked at the wheel and hit the brakes, throwing the van into a controlled skid that ended with the van nose-in at the mouth of the alley, with scant inches to spare on both sides.

Ahead, the lights of the fleeing thieves seemed

much closer. Why were they slowing up? A trick of some kind? Then Joe saw an overturned metal trash bin with a fresh dent in its side. They must have hit it.

He saw his chance. The alley widened into a delivery and loading dock area for the stores on the main street. He pushed the accelerator down all the way. Slowly he drew even with the green van as it sped down the alley. At the instant he nosed ahead, he turned his wheel to the right.

BAM!

The sound of the first impact was loud, but its force wasn't enough to turn the speeding van. Within only seconds to go before they reached the end of the alley and the van had a chance to get away, Joe pulled the wheel hard right again. This time he slammed on the brakes at the same time so that even if they hit him they couldn't move him. The green van hit Joe and bounced into and off the wall. It screeched to a halt as Joe stopped crosswise in front of it, cutting off any chance of escape. Then he jumped out.

"Okay, you guys. Get out of there," he shouted.

Ed and Peter Mason burst from the van like assault troops. They were both wearing the khaki coveralls that the museum's maintenance staff wore. So that's how they did the job, Joe thought to himself. He didn't have time to think exactly what that meant before Ed was charging him.

Ed shouted over his shoulder, "Get his van, Peter, while I take care of this jerk."

Joe's heart sank. His van offered them an easy means of escape, and like an idiot, he'd left the key in the ignition.

"This isn't one of your high school matches, Joe," Ed said. "This is for real and this is when my strength can really make the difference." Ed leapt at him then.

I don't need reminding that this isn't high school wrestling, Joe thought to himself. This is back alley street fighting, and I'll bet I can give you a few surprises.

Waiting until the last possible moment, Joe stepped aside and grabbed Ed by the arm. With his own body as a pivot, he used Ed's momentum to hurl him headfirst toward the brick wall of the building behind him.

When he realized what was happening, Ed gave a shout of protest and tried to bring up a hand to ward off the impact. Too late. He rammed into the wall face-first and collapsed onto the garbage-strewn pavement of the back alley.

Joe whirled and saw Peter fumbling with the door to the Hardy van. "Your turn, turkey!" Joe shouted, lunging at his other opponent. The force of their impact knocked Peter backward against the van. He put up his hands to ward off Joe, but Joe was charged. Adrenaline-pumped, he gave Peter a left to the midsection that doubled him over, then a right to the side of the jaw that bounced his head off the side pillar of the van. Peter's eyes rolled up into his head, and he slowly slumped to the ground.

He wasn't unconscious, Joe realized. He'd better tie up both these guys.

There wasn't any rope in the van, but Joe used a pair of pliers to cut up a pair of jumper cables. They looked like they'd work fine.

Peter was closer. Joe pulled his hands behind his back and wrapped the cable around his wrists, then crossed the alley to deal with the younger brother. Ed was lying on his face, arms akimbo. Joe reached down to pull his hands around his back. As he did, Ed grabbed one of his wrists and used a judo throw to topple him.

Joe scrambled away, but Ed was faster. He planted himself solidly and launched a kick at Joe's head. Joe recoiled, just enough to keep the blow from putting out his lights for good, but still he felt the blackness closing in. The last thing he saw was the gloating face of Ed Mason moving toward him.

Chapter

14

"OKAY, HARDY," ED GROWLED. "You've got this coming."

Joe willed himself to hold on to what little consciousness he had left as Ed grabbed his arm and twisted it viciously. Agony shot through Joe's shoulder, and he used the pain to bring himself to full awareness, to fire his anger. Every muscle and nerve flared to life again. When Ed closed in, Joe exploded upward, smashing his shoulder into Ed Mason's diaphragm. Ed went down, and Joe threw himself on top of him.

Ed made a wild grab for Joe's injured ankle, and Joe felt as if the overmuscled boy had literally torn his foot off. A new wave of fury washed over Joe. He rolled away, then scrambled to his knees and brought his linked hands down on the side of Ed's neck. Ed turned dark red and rolled over, gasping and choking for breath.

Joe seized the moment and wrestled Ed's muscular arms behind his back. Ed tried to resist, but his body wouldn't cooperate. Joe's powerful blow had knocked all the air out of Ed, and he was unable to resist. A few twists of the heavy jumper cable wire and a quick knot, and Ed was immobilized.

After a few deep breaths, Joe rose wearily and got his flashlight from the van. In the back of the Masons' van, he found a large canvas mail sack. He opened it. Even the dim light of the alley revealed the brilliance of clusters of gems on tiaras, necklaces, and rings.

"Okay," Joe said to the two brothers. "I've caught you with the loot. Like father, like sons. You are Richard Courtland's sons, aren't you?"

"That's right. What of it?" Ed replied.

"Where have you got my father and brother?" Joe demanded.

Peter shook his head. "I don't know what you're talking about."

"We don't know anything about your father or your brother, Hardy," Ed added, flopping onto his side and glaring up at his captor. "We figured that your father was still at the museum and that your brother was with you. We're not kidnappers."

"That's right, Joe," Peter said. "We're not criminals at all, really. We simply did this for the challenge of beating you and your father— beating the fabulous Hardys."

Joe stared at him, unbelieving. "You've got tens of millions of dollars in jewels in there, jewels that you just stole from the Bayport Museum. And you say you're not criminals?"

"It's not a question of facts, it's a matter of how you look at the facts," Ed said.

Joe exploded. "Will you just quit it with that nonsense? Now quick—where is my dad? And what have you done with Frank?"

"Look, Joe," Peter said. "We really don't know anything about them. It's the truth."

Joe shook his head, confused. "What about your partner, I mean, your father? Does he have them?"

"He's got nothing to do with any of this," Ed replied quickly. "We pulled off this job entirely by ourselves."

"That's right," Peter said. "Look, Joe, try to understand. Richard Courtland is our father. But when he went to prison, our mom decided to use her maiden name, Mason. She died a few years later, and we were raised by relatives. But Dad stayed in touch with us, all through his years in prison. He was as good a father as he could be from there. And when he was released, he came straight to California to get us, so we could be a family again."

Ed took up the story. "He taught us a lot— not about stealing but about science and technology and how to get things done. But somehow, no matter what we did, we never felt like we were living up to what he wanted from us. So we decided to prove to him that we were worthy of being his sons, by doing what he did—pulling off a really daring and original robbery. Having your dad as an opponent made it even better."

"But it didn't quite work out the way we planned," Peter said. "That's life. Take back the jewels, Joe, and let us go. We'll help you find your father and your brother, we swear."

Joe wished that Vanessa were there to hear this. He could certainly understand wanting to impress a brilliant father. He and Frank had fallen into that psychological trap more than once.

But if Peter and Ed weren't the kidnappers, who was? The obvious candidate was Richard Courtland, but what could Joe do about it?

The sound of sirens split the night. They were coming closer. Someone must have heard the fight and phoned the cops.

"Joe," Peter said urgently. "You're not going to let the cops get us, are you? Sending us to jail would be such a waste."

Joe didn't answer, but he tugged the two brothers over to their van, wrestled them into the back, and climbed in. The keys were in the ignition. Lights off, he carefully backed into the delivery area, turned around, and took off. At the end of the alley, he made a left, away from the sound of the sirens, and drove slowly and carefully. It was close. Two blocks later, a patrol car screamed by going the opposite way, lights flashing.

"Hey, we did it!" Ed exclaimed. "Great work, Hardy."

"Not so fast," Joe snapped. "Whether you clowns know it or not, your father is in this up to his elbows. It's the only thing that can explain my dad and brother disappearing in the middle of all this. And you're going to put me in touch with him, right now. What's his phone number?" He pulled his cellular phone from his pocket, hoping that his recent battle hadn't put it out of commission.

There was a silence that stretched out. Then Peter spoke reluctantly. "He gave us a private number to call in case we ever got in trouble."

"Face it, you just got in trouble," Joe said. "What's the number?"

Peter told him, and Joe thumbed it into the cellular phone. The call was picked up on the fifth ring.

131

"Ed? Peter?" a voice said. "Where are you? What's happened."

Joe recognized Richard Courtland's voice.

"Ed and Peter are in good health, Mr. Courtland," Joe said.

"Who is this?" Courtland demanded.

"Joe Hardy. I've got Ed and Peter tied up in the back of the van, along with most of the crown jewels of Botrovia, which they just stole. I'm on my way to dump the whole package in the laps of the cops."

"No, wait!" Courtland said, his voice rising. "Don't do that."

"Why not?" Joe replied, not bothering to hide his bitterness. "Do you want to tell me what happened to my father and brother?"

There was a long pause at the other end of the line. When Courtland began talking again, he sounded as though he had recovered much of his confidence.

"I'll be glad to talk with you about Frank and your father, Joe," he said. "They're right here with me, and in good health—for now. Apparently when I took them, I paid a couple of installments on my sons' insurance policy, if you catch my meaning."

Joe had to be sure. "Can you prove you've got Frank and Dad?"

"Certainly," Courtland said. "We were just

enjoying a quiet chat. Here, gentlemen, please identify yourselves for our listening audience."

Frank's voice shouted, "Watch yourself, Joe. This guy's got more dirty tricks than you've ever dreamed."

"Don't worry about us," Joe's father added. "You know what to do. Go straight to the police."

Courtland came back on the line. "Ignore them. They're giving you terrible advice, I'm afraid. What I'd like to do is to engineer a little trade. Say the van and its contents—specifically Ed and Peter—in exchange for your father and brother. If you don't want to trade, I'll understand that you don't want to see your brother or father ever again. And I promise you that is something I could make happen."

"I can't let you have the jewels," Joe said. "No way."

Courtland sighed. "No, I didn't suppose you would. Very well. Return them to the museum, if you must. You can claim you found them dumped by the roadside. But in return I want my boys to get away clean. No police, no rumors in the papers, no prosecution, not even any gossip in the halls at school, nothing. Do you agree?"

"I can't control what other people might think or guess," Joe replied. "Or what my dad and Frank do." He would have to play along with Courtland, for the time being.

"I think that I can convince them to go along with my deal by the time you get here," Courtland said with a hint of menace in his voice. "I may have been out of the business for a while, but prison gave me an above-average course in how to be a monster. And I haven't forgotten anything that I learned."

Joe shifted his grip on the phone, which was getting slippery from the sweat on his palm. "Okay, Mr. Courtland. I'll give you back your boys. Where do you want to meet me?"

"Intech," he replied. "Drive past the main building and you'll see a warehouse in the back. My boys know the way."

"I'll be there in fifteen minutes," Joe said, and clicked off.

He glanced over his shoulder and saw that Peter and Ed had been listening closely. Sitting there trussed up, they seemed to be both stunned and relieved. He saw something else, too. A police car, lit up by a streetlight, was pulling onto the road from a side street. For a moment, Joe allowed himself to hope that its appearance was a coincidence. Then the gum ball machine on top of the cruiser began to flash red, and a siren began to wail. The next time Joe dared to glance in his mirror, the police car was only a hundred yards back and quickly closing the gap.

Chapter

15

AS THE CRUISER DREW CLOSER, Joe thought fast. What would Courtland do to Frank and his dad if he felt that Joe had double-crossed him?

"Listen, Hardy," Ed said with a hint of panic in his voice. "This is a terrific set of wheels that can do some astonishing things on the road. I've heard that you're a pretty good driver. Care to show us a little of your stuff?"

Ed's goading angered Joe, but he forced the anger back down and tried to analyze the situation the way he knew his brother would. The highway they were on had two lanes going in each direction. The lanes were divided by a low concrete median, which gave him an idea. He scanned the road ahead and spotted a gap in the wall that was designed to allow service vehicles to cross from one side of the highway to the other. He started to slow down and moved into the right lane, as if about to pull over and stop.

"Joe, do you understand the implications of your actions?" Peter demanded.

"Shut up!" Joe bellowed. "Just be quiet. The last thing I need right now is another distraction."

The officer pulled out to come alongside. At the last possible moment, Joe twisted the wheel left. The van swerved directly into the path of the patrol car. The startled cop slammed on his brakes and swerved to the right to avoid a collision.

As Ed had predicted, the van responded like a race car, throwing itself into a four-wheel drift. As delicately as a surgeon, Joe worked the wheel, aiming the van at the narrow gap in the concrete barrier. The instant the nose of the van was through, he cranked the wheel hard to the left and stomped once on the brakes. Tires screamed in protest, as the heavy van made a perfect bootlegger turn and ended up headed in the opposite direction.

Joe floored the accelerator, then risked a glance back. The patrol car was stopped, its front wheels up on the curb. The two officers were standing beside the car. Joe waited until he was sure he was out of their sight, then turned onto the next side street. After a baffling series of lefts and rights, he charted a course to a back road that he knew would bring him out just a short distance from the Intech plant.

"That's the place," Peter said. The van's headlights showed a one-story aluminum-sided building, about thirty feet wide by twenty deep, with a high, wide, overhead door in the center of the long side.

Joe pulled up with the nose of the van almost touching the door. He set the parking brake but left the engine running.

Looking into the back, he said, "What is this place?"

"It's a warehouse," Peter replied. "Dad's been letting us use it for a work space."

Joe sat for a moment and considered the situation. The building was dark and quiet. Should he honk to let Courtland know they had arrived? It didn't seem like the best idea so he decided to let his fingers do the walking. He picked up the cellular phone again and said, "What was that emergency number again?"

Courtland answered halfway through the first ring. "We're here," Joe told him.

"So I see," Courtland replied. "Now it's just a matter of making our little exchange. It's cold out there so I'll raise the door to the loading area, and you can pull your van inside."

The overhead door started to move.

Joe sensed a trap. "I don't know. . . ."

Courtland sighed heavily. "Oh, please," he said. "I was quite frank with you on Saturday. I want no part of crime anymore. I'm quite happy with my life as it is. All I want is to keep a couple of high-spirited youngsters from getting into trouble with the law. I really do not want to do anything that might send me to prison again. I mean that sincerely. So do us all a favor and come in out of the cold."

Joe thought for a moment, then said, "I'll compromise, and pull in halfway."

Courtland laughed sourly. "A typical compromise—instead of coming in out of the cold, you let the cold in here. Very well. Let's get this over with."

Joe eased the van forward into the lighted space. Then he climbed out and slid open the side door.

"Here they are, Courtland," he announced. "Now how about your end of the bargain."

"They're right here," Courtland replied, opening the door to a small side room. "Off you go, my friends. I've enjoyed having your company, but I much prefer that of my boys."

Fenton and Frank, hands bound, walked through the doorway and stood blinking at the light.

"Okay. Your turn, guys," said Joe. He pulled

the Masons out of the van and untied their legs. The moment they were free, they hurried over to their father's side. He produced a small knife and started to cut their bonds. Joe untied the hands of his father and brother.

" 'All's well that ends well,' as the poet says," Courtland observed. Joe noticed that he had a small electronic control device in his hand. "Fenton, I'll be gracious and offer the resignation to you this time," Courtland continued. "You won, just as you did in our last chess game. Thanks to your quite remarkable son Joe. Now, if you would be so good as to depart and leave us be. Take those jewels back to the museum, and we'll forget the whole unfortunate affair."

Fenton Hardy shook his head. "I'm sorry, Courtland. I can't do that. Your sons broke the law, and so did you. I'm going to have to report you to the authorities."

"Come, come, Hardy," Courtland protested. "No real harm's been done. Justice has been served."

"Your concept of justice, perhaps," Fenton replied. "A concept that allows you or those like you to do anything they want as long as no one catches you. Your 'justice' holds the law in contempt. I've never been able to live like that before and I don't plan to start now, Courtland."

"You are a difficult man, Fenton Hardy. Oh

139

well." A look of resignation passed over Courtland's face. He pressed a button and the door slammed down onto the roof of the van, so hard that it made a dent at least six inches deep and pinned the van in place. There would be no escape that way, Joe saw.

Courtland grinned. "You've forced my hand, I'm afraid. The boys and I are simply going to have to take those millions of dollars' worth of jewels and make ourselves scarce. So much for the honest life. I'll look back on it with regret, from a beach somewhere in South America."

"That does sound attractive," Peter said.

"Yeah, way to go, Dad," Ed added.

Courtland looked over at them. "You know, boys, I never realized how much you mean to me until I thought I might lose you. I won't let that happen, whatever it takes."

"I'm sorry, Courtland," Fenton said. "We can't let you go and certainly not with the crown jewels. Face the facts and come peacefully. Any resistance will just make matters worse for all of you."

"You'll have to take us," Courtland retorted.

"We will," Fenton said. "Come on, boys. Don't worry, they're not armed."

"Not with guns, true," Peter said. He pulled a box down from a nearby shelf and took out three gas masks. Handing two to his father and brother, he added, "But we do have the help of friends."

From an obscure corner of the room, five robots rolled rapidly into sight. They were bigger than the ones Joe had seen at school. They paused in the center of the room. Then, as Peter manipulated the controls on the pad in his hand, they turned and raced toward the Hardys.

"Intruders!" they shrieked, as they began to spray streams of a whitish gas. *"Intruders!"*

Chapter

16

As THE GAS-SPRAYING ROBOTS raced toward the Hardys, Frank said, "I think I've been here before." He looked quickly around and spotted a length of metal pipe. He grabbed it and said, "Time for a little creative reprogramming."

Holding his jacket over his nose with his left hand, Frank made a one-handed swing at the lead robot. It swayed and stopped, then began scooting toward the left side of the room, shrieking, " 'Trud, 'trud!'' A feet feet later, it collided with another of the robots. The sound of the crash was like the clatter of two garbage cans being blown down a hill.

Joe avoided a clumsy blow from one of the robots. Coughing, he rolled on the floor to the side of the room and crashed into a pile of lumber. He groped through it and found a two-by-four about as long as a baseball bat. As he stumbled to his feet, another robot rolled in his direction, one of its arms—one that ended in a spinning circular saw—raised to attack him.

Joe was suddenly in the batter's box, score tied, bottom of the ninth, three and two, with three runners on base. He put everything into his swing. The two-by-four caught the robot in its sheet metal midsection and knocked it right off its wheels. Delicate electronic components went flying across the room in a clatter of broken pieces. Joe dusted off his hands, then turned to help the rest of his team.

Courtland was standing at the side of the overhead door, tugging at a loop of chain. Joe suddenly realized that he meant to free the van and use it for his escape with the loot still in the back.

"Don't let them get away," Fenton shouted as Ed and Peter dashed for the van.

"Hey, Joe!" Frank yelled. "This way, quick!"

Joe instantly saw what his brother meant. He sprinted across the room, directly in front of the two robots that were still operating. The robots turned to pursue him and ran directly into the path of Peter and Ed.

"Not us, you traitors," Ed shouted, raising

his arm to shield his face from a robotic hammer blow.

"Ed, it can't tell who we are," Peter said desperately. "When I'm not on the remote control, they're programmed to attack anything that moves. We just have to run for it. Aarrgh!"

One of the robots hit him in the side with a wrench, then sprayed gas at him.

Frank didn't wait to find out how this fight would end. He sprinted past Courtland to the door of the van, reached inside, and jerked out the ignition key. He flung the key into the darkness.

"I'll get you for that," Courtland threatened. He grabbed Frank's jacket and pulled back his right arm for a punch to the face. Before it landed, though, Fenton tackled him. The boys saw that he had not forgotten the lessons he'd taken many years ago. It took only a few well-placed blows from Fenton to subdue his rival.

Peter lay on the ground, getting pummeled by one of his own creations. "Turn it off, turn it off," he pleaded. "The remote's on the bench!"

Joe hurried back to the bench and found the device. He pushed a red button, and silence descended. Keeping the control in his hand, he took out the cellular phone and dialed the Bayport Police Department.

"Sorry we got you into this, Dad," Ed said as they heard the distant sound of sirens.

Richard Courtland rubbed his head and tried to smile. "You still pack quite a punch, Fenton." He turned to his sons. "That's all right, boys. Let's just say we've finally gotten to know one another, eh?"

"We're going to jail, aren't we, Dad?" Ed asked.

"I'm afraid it's rather likely." His half-smile turned into an expression of cold menace as he took in Frank and Joe. "But let's just put it this way, boys. The people who've put us there have also given us a strong reason to get out as quickly as possible. We may have the last laugh yet."

"Unlikely, Courtland," Fenton said. "And I wouldn't try it."

The opening night of the exhibition was glorious.

All the spectators were dressed in their very best. Conversations buzzed throughout the room, except near the display cases. Those who went over to examine the artistry of the gem-studded jewelry fell silent in awe.

James Abrahamson was standing with the Hardys near the entrance to the gallery. "Thanks for helping me achieve the dream of a lifetime, you three," he said. "You may not know it, but my grandfather was a renowned jeweler in Botrovia before he came to America. For all I know, some of the pieces in this collection are his work.''

Fenton looked at him in surprise. "I never knew you were of Botrovian descent.''

"I suppose it never came up,'' Abrahamson replied. "But, yes. I even helped, in a very minor way, to speed the country's liberation. After that, the chance to sponsor this exhibition was too good to pass up. You can understand why I was so anxious about all the problems were were having. I'm afraid you probably thought *I* was one of the problems.''

They laughed. Then Frank said, "There was even a point when we wondered if you might be planning to steal the jewels.''

Abrahamson stood silent for a moment, then nodded. "I can see why my actions might have seemed suspicious. I just wish I'd paid as much attention to those infernal trash cans as I did to the other aspects of security. I daresay I stuck my nose into the wrong places at the wrong times. I can be a little overbearing.''

"Well, everything worked out all right,'' Frank said. "And I think this exhibition will accomplish what you wanted.''

"Congratulations,'' Joe added.

"Ah, excuse me,'' Abrahamson said with an affable nod. "I just noticed a reporter from one of the New York newspapers.''

As he walked away, Frank said, "Now that

the jewels are safe, I bet he's happy for all the extra publicity. It does make quite a story."

"Boy, what a bunch," Joe added. "I hate to think what might have happened if Courtland and his sons had actually worked together from the beginning."

Fenton Hardy shook his head. "Well, I'll pay more attention to you two in the future, that's for sure. You were quite right to suspect them, after all."

Vanessa walked over to Joe. "I have a feeling it's my turn to apologize," she said softly. "Although I don't think I'll ever forget the sight of you doing somersaults in my salsa. You were right—mostly—and I was wrong—mostly. Will that do?"

She kissed him on the cheek. Joe reached out to give her a quick hug, then stopped when he noticed Callie watching them with a smile on her face. Joe felt his cheeks growing warm.

Callie tucked her arm in Frank's. "I think we should all probably apologize," she said lightly. "How could we all be taken in by such a pair of phonies?"

"Those guys have probably worked half their lives learning to sound that sincere," Joe said.

"I just hope this experience ends up putting them straight," Frank said.

"No, you don't," Joe said with a wink. "You'd love to cross swords with them again."

"Well, I've had a lifetime's worth of Richard Courtland," their father said. "He beat me once. And he and his sons almost did it a second time. They would have, except for *my* sons." He put an arm around Frank's and Joe's shoulders and added, "I'll do very nicely without another rematch."

"Except for chess?" Frank suggested.

Fenton nodded. "Except for chess. In fact, I wouldn't be surprised if I get a letter from Courtland, suggesting a game by mail."

"Mr. Hardy," Callie said. "How did Richard Courtland kidnap you?"

"Simple. He just called me up and said he had information for me. I met him at his house, and he knocked me out and tied me up."

"But why did he get involved?" Frank asked.

"He figured out what Ed and Peter were up to and decided to help by covering for any mistakes they might make."

"We'll be sure to appreciate our boyfriends more in the future," said Callie. "Oafish as they occasionally are."

"We may not be the smoothest, but at least we're honest," Joe protested. He pulled out a pack of gum and offered it around, then took a stick himself.

"I can't get over the fact that two such bright, promising boys could turn so bad," Laura Hardy said, joining them.

"It's a matter of the wrong kind of father figure," Callie suggested. "From what you all have told me, they idolized their father. They don't see wrong and right as moral questions. Like their dad, they tend to see morality as a big game. And they wanted to show their father they could play that game and win."

Vanessa frowned. "I still don't understand how Ed and Peter got those robots disguised as trash cans into the museum."

"Surprisingly easily," Joe said. "The same maintenance firm that services Intech services the museum. The Masons got part-time jobs with the service and used their cover to roll in their robots."

"Which also explains how they were able to pull off the robbery," Frank added. "They were helping to clean the museum that night."

"But if they were already inside," Vanessa continued, "why did they even bother with the robots?"

"Those robots were the only way to set off false alarms without being detected," Joe explained.

"How did they work?" Callie asked.

Frank had the answer for that one. "I finally got to look at a couple today. Very sophisticated, but Peter's work would not have been possible without access to the robotronics division of Jax Industries. Those robots were

149

remote-controlled by using TV screens and joysticks in the van outside the museum. They were also equipped with directable lasers that Ed and Peter used to set off the wall alarms.''

"But couldn't the Jax stuff be traced back to them?" said Vanessa.

"Not necessarily," Joe replied. "It's sold all over. Anyway, I think they kept telling themselves that this was more of a prank than a crime. Personally, I think they would have kept the jewels, but we'll never know.''

"One thing I know," Vanessa said. "I'm ready for that pizza you promised me, Joe."

Joe grinned. "Sounds good to me. Frank, Callie?"

"Sure," the two said in unison. Then Callie added, "What about you, Mr. and Mrs. Hardy?"

"Why, thank you, Callie," Laura said with a smile. "But Fenton owes me a nice, romantic dinner, and I don't care to share him.''

"Some place without alarms," Fenton added, winking at his sons. "And totally unautomated."

As the four turned to go, Joe discovered that he was still holding his gum wrapper. He took a step in the direction of the trash receptacle near the entrance, then stopped himself.

"No," he said. "On second thought, I'll just keep it in my pocket."

Frank and Joe's next case:

Frank and Joe's friend Ben Martin has just hit the jackpot in the state lottery. His prize: a cool five million dollars' worth of pure danger! Ben's about to discover that sudden wealth can be a sure ticket to disaster . . . because there's nothing like cold, hard cash to bring out the cold-hearted schemes of a greedy, criminal mind.

The high cost of living has already taken a toll—Ben's sister Emily has been kidnapped for a king's ransom. From small-time hustlers to big-time operators, just about everyone's looking for a piece of the action, and the Hardys have no trouble finding suspects. The trick is getting to Emily and getting her home before she pays the highest price of all . . . in *Winner Take All*, Case #85 in The Hardy Boys Casefiles™.